# Lake Effect

stories

## Dayle Furlong

Cormorant Books

Copyright © 2022 Dayle Furlong
This edition copyright © 2022 Cormorant Books Inc.

No part of this publication may be reproduced, stored in a retrieval system or transmitted, in any form or by any means, without the prior written consent of the publisher or a licence from The Canadian Copyright Licensing Agency (Access Copyright). For an Access Copyright licence, visit www.accesscopyright.ca or call toll free 1.800.893.5777.

  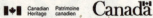 

We acknowledge financial support for our publishing activities: the Government of Canada, through the Canada Book Fund and The Canada Council for the Arts; the Government of Ontario, through the Ontario Arts Council, Ontario Creates, and the Ontario Book Publishing Tax Credit. We acknowledge additional funding provided by the Government of Ontario and the Ontario Arts Council to address the adverse effects of the novel coronavirus pandemic.

**LIBRARY AND ARCHIVES CANADA CATALOGUING IN PUBLICATION**

Title: Lake effect : stories / Dayle Furlong.
Names: Furlong, Dayle, author.
Identifiers: Canadiana (print) 20190230800 | Canadiana (ebook) 20190230797 | ISBN 9781770865723 (softcover) | ISBN 9781770865730 (HTML)
Classification: LCC PS8611.U75 L35 2022 | DDC C813/.6—dc23

United States Library of Congress Control Number: 2022934285

Cover Art: Angel Guerra, Archetype
Interior text design: Tannice Goddard, tannicegdesigns.ca
Printer: Friesens

Printed and bound in Canada.

CORMORANT BOOKS INC.
260 SPADINA AVENUE, SUITE 502, TORONTO, ON M5T 2E4
www.cormorantbooks.com

*For B & B*

*... the Great Lakes seem everlasting and so,
in the space of a single lifetime, they are.*
— PIERRE BERTON

*The Lake is us.*
— GORD DOWNIE

# Contents

Tributaries / 1

Skin Island / 17

Lake Effect / 31

Shoreline / 51

The Fresh Coast / 63

Ebb / 81

Muddying the Waters / 95

A Duck to Water / 119

Differential Settlement / 131

Adamantine / 149

The Pier / 173

What Follows the Falls / 183

Acknowledgements / 203

# *Tributaries*

THE BLOCKAGE HAD BEEN disregarded as trash: a cluster of plastic bags, a few water bottles, and what looked like a discarded red jacket, swollen with water, caught in a bushel of cattails. When Constable Belmont realized that it was not junk but another body, bloated and decomposing, three days had passed. The boy floated face down, head and limbs immersed in the river. When fire services pulled him out of the McIntyre River, Belmont couldn't look at the boy's face, afraid he would recognize it. The boy had his mother's eyes.

THE FIRST TIME BELMONT saw Pamela, weighing baggage at Thunder Bay Airport's North Star Airlines check-in counter, he wanted to touch her heart-shaped face, smell her glossy hair. He didn't look like a cop; otherwise, she'd said later, she'd never have gone out with him in the first place. He took her to Lot 66 and ordered an expensive bottle of wine, which he quickly cancelled when she told him she didn't drink.

He ordered coffee. His hands shook under the table. He hadn't dated anyone since Glenda left him, ten years earlier.

"Pan seared Lake-of-the-Woods pickerel, please."

And when the pickerel came, they laughed at the small chunk

of fish underneath a dollop of cream sauce topped with a sprig of parsley.

"Too fancy," he said.

She told him her ex-husband cooked pickerel in beer batter. She blurted it out, trying to hide her shame; she felt uncomfortable acknowledging her ex because Belmont knew who he was, everyone in law enforcement did. He was "known to the police" as the newspapers said.

"My daughter Shy-Anne was just accepted into law school, and my son Lionel, a tadpole since birth — he demanded to swim in Lake Superior when he was just two — is a competitive swimmer," she told him.

Belmont didn't know what to say. He had his suspicions about the swim coach; everyone did, but no one could prove anything. The only thing he'd noticed was that most of the boys who trained with him were troubled or disruptive, lost. Without having met Lionel, Belmont immediately felt protective. He told Pamela what he thought about the coach. She said that Lionel hadn't mentioned anything and dismissed it as malicious gossip coming from rival swim coaches. He figured she knew better than anyone.

Over the next few months, he'd kept his courtship discreet. He'd show up at the airport in uniform, buy Pamela a coffee from the Tim Hortons upstairs. Slip her a pack of chocolate-covered almonds, the novelty ones called Moose Droppings, from the souvenir shop. They grew into one another slowly and gently, cautious of each other's scars. The scars grafted onto his body from his wife's abandonment, the etchings of betrayals and losses recorded on her face by a man who proclaimed love but wouldn't, or couldn't, deliver. The first time they made love,

Belmont went to the bathroom afterward to shower under hot water just to stop the trembling.

THE MORNING THE PROVINCIAL police found another boy's body in the river, Belmont filed his report at the station and drove straight home. He almost hit a mother pushing a stroller through an intersection. His hands were sweating on the steering wheel. He needed to get off the road. He didn't know how much more of this he could stand. He feared that one day the boy would be Lionel. He turned into the driveway of his red-brick bungalow, built in 1962, in the Edgewater neighbourhood. With a mug of fresh-brewed coffee in hand, he sat under the black spruce in his backyard, the tree's brittle limbs tightly clustered, grass sloping toward the riverbank like a bolt of green velvet. He watched the Neebing River, thin and brown, flow towards the floodway and the lake. The late spring's morning sun flooded the river with sable light that contrasted with the dark shadows that purled on the surface. His breath slowed. He felt a slight measure of peace. He spotted a doe and her two fawns on the opposite shore. A twig snapped behind him. The little family leapt into the forest. Startled, he turned to see Pam in his backyard, beckoning him to come.

WHEN BELMONT WAS A boy, his next-door neighbour stood on her front step every day after school, holding out her arms for a hug.

"Hungry?" Lorraine would ask.

He would nod and she would shepherd him into her home, taking his packsack, emptying his lunch bag, and inserting tomorrow's lunch. She would regularly feed him moose stew, a chunk of bread and a cup of tea brimming with milk and sugar to replace the supper she knew Belmont's mother wouldn't be making him.

Lorraine's house smelled of the cinnamon candles she burned to get the stink of the paper mill off her husband's shirts. She had four children and considered Belmont her fifth. He'd play with Lorraine's kids, usually building things with Lego, until his own mother, housecoat askew, bottle of vodka in her wide pocket, turned up at Lorraine's front door to collect him home to make her something to eat.

Lorraine's husband was from Cape Breton. She met him in Toronto while studying early childhood education. He was in Ontario looking for work. Moved with her back to Thunder Bay and found work at the mill. Pregnancy and child-rearing kept her at home. He was gone most nights after work, drinking at the tavern until last call.

Lorraine was the one who went to Belmont's parent-teacher interviews. She looked after him in the summer. She brought him along with her children to the parks and the lakefront, walked them down the hills of a sand dune succession she'd discovered, warm beige sand sprouting thick blades of grass.

Sometimes Belmont felt awkward, out of place, foolish for being there. He was an outsider, not really part of her family. When gripped by uncertainty he stood by himself on those trips to the lake, her kids fighting over a bag of nuts or the last can of Coke. He wondered why she cared so much, when his own mother didn't.

Late one night he heard her through the open window telling her husband that she considered him her adopted son. Her husband snorted. She told him that the boy had no one to look after him and that he needed her.

"Not worth caring about other people's children. You raise them and they'll forget you," he said.

Belmont promised himself he wouldn't ever forget her.

At his graduation at Confederation College, he waited for her to come. "I'll be sitting right in front," Lorraine had said. A newly minted graduate of the Police Foundations program, he kept watching the door, anticipating her arrival. He was worried that he'd missed her. She must have stayed home. The sky was heavy with clouds. It was cold enough to snow.

"Serve and Protect," the invited speaker, a Staff Sergeant from the Thunder Bay Police Services said. "We are like tributaries, small rivers that contribute water to large lakes, always serving something bigger. We serve the community, promote peace, and prevent crime. Serve it over ourselves, our families, our friends. Let nothing impede you as you serve. All of us, no matter our station — constables, security guards, and corrections officers — are all called to serve something bigger than ourselves."

The speech inspired Belmont. He couldn't wait to serve. As long as he could remember, he'd wanted to be a police officer. Other boys wanted to be firemen. But not Belmont. He wanted to be someone with authority, someone people looked up to.

He waited for Lorraine on the stairs outside for an hour after the ceremony ended and the buffet dinner had been served in the gym. But she didn't come. He gave up waiting and left with his fellow graduates to stay out all night drinking. When he got home the following morning, there was a police car in Lorraine's driveway. He stood on the street, just staring at it.

"Dumb woman got herself killed," his mother said, swaying in the doorway.

CONSTABLE BELMONT HANDED SERGEANT Whyte a hot coffee.

"A mother of two young kids, taking a shortcut home out by the college," Whyte said, "beaten to a pulp out by McIntyre. Jumped and robbed. Left for dead."

Belmont swallowed his coffee. Lorraine had been found, all those years ago, down by the river, beaten to death. Later that day two boys were caught trying to use her credit card at the mall.

"Didn't expect to find her when out looking for kids," Whyte said.

"I've heard what the kids are using now raises their body temperature sky-high," an officer said. "Only natural they'd want to cool down, go for a late-night swim."

Belmont couldn't remain quiet. He couldn't let this bit of gossip pass for a valid explanation.

"I've heard there's a truck driver targeting the community."

"We don't know for sure what's going on," Whyte said. "This city ain't safe anymore."

Thunder Bay had never been safe. From the start, it was a town full of traders and prospectors and eventually hard-scrabble boys hungry for industrial work. It flourished under the fur trade, followed by many prosperous years of silver mining, and when the silver veins gave out, the way was made for grain elevators, then sawmills, and the Great Lakes Paper Company — the largest pulp and paper manufacturing facility in the world, a business that still produces, despite worldwide market decline for paper products. A city that, on the surface, seemed capable of nothing more innocuous than the banter between Port Arthur and Fort William, debating the merits of amalgamation and a mayor in Port Arthur running for candidacy in Fort William in order to expand his governance. A city that, since the 1880s, had flooded in the spring, rivers tearing homes and bridges from their foundations, carrying them through town, until a floodway was built almost a hundred years later.

"Belmont?" Sergeant Whyte said and gestured to the open door, shepherding the officers inside the meeting room, "You with us? We've got a lot to go over."

"I DON'T CARE WHAT the police say," Pam said.

"We'll wait for the boy's toxicology report and we'll know for sure," Belmont said.

"I don't need no report. A serial killer is throwing those children in the lake. And I'm sleepless waiting for mine to show up."

"We don't know for sure, honey."

"No? Well then you wait. I'm going to look for my son."

Belmont watched her put a bottle of water and a sandwich in her purse.

"Those kids knew water. None of them would have drowned unless someone held them under," she said.

"We can't just assume it's homicide."

"You're not going to investigate the possibility?"

Belmont shook his head.

She pushed her tears away with the back of her hand and ordered him to leave. Belmont left. Outside he watched the kids in the neighbourhood. They had their eyes on the cellphones in their hands, unaware of Belmont. Eight, ten, eleven years old at the most. A world away from how he'd grown up; smarter, more inquisitive, more in touch with the outside world. Could he make the city safe for them? He couldn't even protect his son — yes, his son — that's how he'd come to think of Lionel. As his. Belmont had been there when his own father hadn't. He'd showed up at his science fairs and had volunteered for pizza day lunches — without any sleep, after a long night shift where he'd been spit on, cursed at, and kicked for breaking up bar fights and domestics. He'd even begun setting aside money for Lionel to go to college. He'd tried once to get him to talk about the swim coach, but Lionel wouldn't say a thing; rage-fuelled and rebellious, he'd stormed out of the house, knocking over the kids from next door on his way down the sidewalk. He'd come back, no matter how long he'd been gone. Three days? Nothing for him. Belmont would wake up to find that his wallet and Pam's purse had been raided. They knew he was out with friends doing what he wanted. Not going to school.

Hanging out down by the river.

From inside Belmont heard Pam's sobs.

HE HADN'T CRIED WHEN he saw the cruiser outside Lorraine's door. He walked inside and called her name, disbelieving what he'd heard his mother say, *That dumb woman got herself killed.* An officer, with kind blue eyes, asked, "Do you know these children?" His black eyebrows narrowed in concern. The kids ran to Belmont.

"I'm her son," Belmont said.

He remembers now, standing outside Pam's door, what Lorraine's husband had said the summer before she was killed. "You will raise him as your own, and then he'll forget about you." Belmont was indignant when he'd heard that; he knew that he'd never let Lorraine down. He was her adopted son. He loved her, the soft way she smelled, her cooking, her comfortable sofa, the soft shag rug. Her no-nonsense hands and her laugh, the way she sang, and her gift for mimicry. The way she fussed over him and made sure his schoolwork was done. Loved her pride, her refusal to wallow, or accept charity. She took what was left of her husband's paycheque and stocked the fridge, tended to her garden, made soups and stews and froze them for when there wasn't anything through the winter months.

HE WOULDN'T FORGET ABOUT Lionel. He had to find out where he was, even if he took on unpaid hours, breached protocol, and looked into the files alone. He'd find something. He'd find out for sure where he was. That evening at the start of his shift, he drove by his childhood home in Current River, sold to a young family when his mother ran off to Minneapolis with a man she met online, and parked close by.

The owner of his old house, a young stay-at-home mom, saw the cruiser through the window and emerged moments later with coffee in hand. She walked briskly, chunky glasses over bright blue eyes, trim body clothed in cranberry leggings and a hot pink racer back.

She knocked on the car window.

"I used to live here," he said.

"The neighbours mentioned you did. You want to come inside and have a look?"

Belmont shook his head. No, he couldn't go inside. That would be too much to bear; just looking at his father's old work shed and the basketball net over the door brought back memories of his father. Memories of the evening he tucked Belmont into bed and never came home. He had worked night shifts at the pulp mill — the "midnight lumber shift" he called it — for a company, flush with money, mindful of a community, full of hope. A primary obliterator of the land, or so said the tree-planters from the south, who rode through Northwestern Ontario in their cars, crying at the deforestation. Who'd one day obtain comfortable white-collar jobs, tenure track positions at universities or as heads of government ministries, while Belmont's father the night-shift security guard, fed his family by guarding what they called slaughter. Belmont imagined his father's last night, as he constantly did, while the stay-at-home mom passed a blue ceramic mug of coffee through the open window.

His father's coffee might not have been hot. He'd have been making his rounds, checking the pulp mills for intruders. All his training dictated keeping close watch for would-be thieves, burly men, hungry for shortcuts to profit, but even as a young kid Belmont knew his father would only find boys, thrill-seekers, climbing or sliding down yellow mountains of sawdust.

Belmont pictured his father getting out of the work-issued, mud-splattered, grey truck, walking toward the mill with a flashlight in hand. Would he have made his rounds the way Belmont now patrols neighbourhoods? Cruising through the city at the beginning of a shift, when all was still quiet, driving the streets, alleys, and a downtown core he knew like the back of his hand. Mindlessly patrolling the grounds, processing details the way he also noticed a neighbour's habits: the blinds pulled down at the same time every afternoon, the smell of dinner cooking at five, the timings of comings and goings, and lights out at night so regular the routine became barely noticeable.

Perhaps that's why he didn't see the crane. The company had started repairing the kraft mill. The crane truck was parked nearby. Somehow the jib had gotten loose; it fell on Belmont's father. The police officers pounding on the door got his mother out of bed. He watched her from his room as the police spoke to her. She listened. One of the officers reached out to hold her elbow. She didn't move. "Do you want us to come in?" he asked. She said she didn't think so and said nothing more. "Will you be okay, Dawn?" His mother said yes, thanked the officers, and closed the door. Belmont ran back to bed, not yet knowing that his mother was coming to tell him that their lives would be changed forever.

"Officer?" The woman was still standing by his car. "Are you okay?"

"Yes," Belmont responded. He noticed the mug of coffee in his hands. He tried to return it to the woman through the open window.

"Hang on to it. Bring it back next time you're in the neighbourhood."

BELMONT HELD PAM ON the sofa in her living room, six weeks ago, just before Lionel went missing. She lived on the shores of the Kaministiquia River, just west of Thunder Bay. She'd won a poker game at the casino and had made a down payment on the house. A place with floor to ceiling windows, vaulted ceilings, and a wood stove. She kept two horses in a small barn behind the house.

Shy-Anne puttered around in the kitchen making dinner. Belmont found the smell of moose stew comforting. The parsnips and carrots boiling on the stove steamed up the windows. Birthday presents, gift-bags covered with tufts of tissue paper, sticking out like a cedar waxwing's crest, piled on the chair. Lionel's seventeenth birthday and the boy hadn't bothered to show up. They'd waited for three hours, long past the time he'd said he'd be there. Dusk fell. Pam grew restless.

Through the window Belmont saw that the spring storm that had whipped the house with mushy snow pellets all afternoon had finally settled. Pam's mares snorted in the barn behind the house.

"Horse ride before supper?" she asked.

After putting on their leather gear, Belmont led the animals, cocoa and moss scents emanating from their bodies, outside. The young mares stamped their hooves in the cold. The clouds had dissipated and a circus of iridescent green northern lights emerged. Belmont's breath, thick as cotton, dispersed above his head, mixed with vapour from the horses' snouts.

Belmont and Pam mounted their horses. He watched her pelvis rock in the saddle and wanted her.

"If only he'd go back to school."

"Give him purpose," Belmont said.

"I should've kept him in his room and locked the door."

"You've got to let him make his own choices."

"He shouldn't have quit swimming. He should have told me."

After the First General Grand Prix swim meet he came home and threw his Speedo in the garbage. Earlier that afternoon he'd swum the one-hundred metre breast stroke, powering and pulling his way up and down his lane, leaving slower swimmers in his wake. When he finished, he turned and watched the other swimmers finish their races. But, as he hung on to the lane rope and heaved, the coach approached. He'd been disqualified. He hadn't touched the wall with both hands.

Pam had assumed that's why he'd quit swimming. Precipitating a downward spiral of depression that compelled him to leave school and stop talking to any of his friends, the kids who didn't go to the river, kids he'd known all his life.

"I'm not the first mother to go through this," she said.

"And you won't be the last," Belmont said.

"My good, fine child has lost his way."

They watched the lake in silence. In late March, Superior's

shoreline was ragged with ice; the blue water looked falsely safe, cool and inviting, but it was ice-cold. It promised nothing but pleasure. A carefree swim, cool water against warm skin, the joy of weightlessness, that surge of power, a sense of invincibility. For Pam, water more often meant getting up early to drive him to practice, prepping food for his disciplined diet and watching him train so hard that the effort left his lungs searing. He once told her that after a race it felt like his alveoli were being pricked by shards of glass.

They dismounted the horses, took off their clothes and sat in the sauna hut. As soon as they were hot, skin as red as newborns, they went outside and lay down in the snow. Flakes flew like horse spittle around them.

WHEN LIONEL STOPPED COMING home, Pam became distant and immobile. She didn't want to talk to Belmont or anyone for that matter; she wouldn't answer her phone or return messages. She hadn't tended to her horses, Shy-Anne said when Belmont called. She told him that reporters from Toronto were hounding Pam, calling day and night, sending emails and text messages, communicating improbable things: *We're behind you and the community all the way.*

"They think they know what my mom needs?" Shy-Anne said and begged him to come and check up on Pam.

He said he would.

AND NOW, THIS MORNING, thinking about and longing for her, remembering her hips and the warmth of her breasts as he held her on the couch a month and a half ago, he drove out to see her. He had news. The detective assigned to the case told him they were going to expand the scope of the investigation due to a witness who'd seen a person of interest with one of the boys who'd drowned. He was someone known to police.

Just after six in the morning, Belmont finished his night shift. He knew Pam would be getting up for work. A beautiful morning, mauve streaks of sun across a royal blue sky, wiry birch branches, black and leafless, encircled her house, the chimney spouting grey plumes of smoke. Belmont parked the cruiser, ascended the steps, and saw a number of flower bouquets, a pie in a Tupperware container, another one with cupcakes. He presumed these were gestures of support from neighbours and colleagues from the airline. None of them touched. Belmont knocked, but there was no answer.

He went around back and knocked on the patio door. He pressed his face up to the glass. Inside, curled together on the couch were Pam and her ex-husband. Belmont was stunned. How long had this been going on? When had he come back around? And why would she choose him? She hated him — or so she said. A con artist, always up to no good, involved with online fraud, she'd said. And now he was curled around her, their bodies partially covered by the green plaid blanket Belmont had bought her at the County Fair Plaza for Christmas.

In Pamela's face Belmont saw Lionel's eyes, mouth and lips, and in the body holding her, a replica of Lionel's wiry frame. He wondered if she was seeking some semblance of her son in his arms or if she was punishing herself. Was she lying to herself? Did she think she could excuse his lying, oft-repeated attempts at draining her bank accounts, his inability to keep a job longer than six months? Yes? Just to have yet another go-round?

Belmont would never hurt her like that.

A twig snapped. He turned to see a stag, a hundred yards away, large antlers and proud head held high on a firm neck. The beast had the same sensitive eyes as the doe and fawns crossing the river he'd watched in his backyard, gentleness belied by the sheer size of his crown. From across the distance, they watched one another in silence.

Belmont acquiesced. This was her family, not his; her home and life to do with as she pleased. He moved to the front of the house, started his car, backed out of the driveway, tires spitting gravel as they hit the unpaved country road, and took one last look. She was standing in the kitchen window now, eyes hollow and mournful. Belmont floored the pedal and sped back to the city.

At the station, tired and filled with rage, he cornered the detective on the case, "I don't want any more information," he said and even though it broke his heart, he didn't want to serve. He didn't want to be involved in the search. Lionel wasn't his son. He couldn't call himself his father, not now. He didn't want to let him go, but he would. He had to.

# Skin Island

THE SAILOR IN THE distance hoists his sail and the boat scuds toward Skin Island. Plump clouds hang over towering black spruce and copper chunks of Precambrian shield that jut from the forest floor like crystal formations. Although I find it inexpressibly beautiful, I still blame that island. It's why I watch the sailor now. The island changed our lives. It's the reason we rarely see Jesse. I don't blame him for staying away. Some things you just can't tell a soul.

It was warm the weekend Jesse came home from college. Close to twenty years it's been. I was only fifteen then. On the day of his arrival, a clear morning in early May, Grant and I were cleaning the sailboat. Grant's friends called his little blue boat with yellow trim a *hooker*. In sailing terms that meant a vessel that's *come down a bit*. Owning something lacklustre wasn't Grant's, my stepfather's, habit. He owned one of the nicest houses in Marathon, a town on the banks of Lake Superior nestled into the curves of the most treacherous section of the Trans-Canada Highway. Dangerous chunks of rock frequently broke free from cliffs and fell onto the road. A charging moose could total a car in one unexpected moment. The beautiful scenery, the middle of the boreal forest of robust evergreens and a rocky shoreline stretching as far as the eye could see, belied the menacing geography.

Grant loved that boat. He held on to it the way he held on to Mom and me, as if we were gold sifted from a cold and unforgiving river. He met Mom when we lived in the row houses next to the pulp mill. (The mill closed a while back and the smokestack was torn down only last year.) Back then it wasn't the prettiest part of town. Heavy machinery groaned night and day. The putrid rotten-egg smell, emissions from that smokestack, wafted over the town, but was strongest just outside our windows.

Grant and his thirteen-year-old son Jesse moved to town when mining families from all over the world — drawn to the area by Hemlo Gold Mines, the richest deposits in the world — were building houses and businesses and schools and roads. Back then I was twelve. I was resentful of the new families who had much more than we did. I was especially resentful of Grant. He made my mother laugh so loud — something I had never heard before. Finding out that my mother had a robust sense of humour wasn't something I wanted to find out through his pathetic jokes. I ambushed her one evening, made a snide point of asking if she thought Grant would marry someone with a child. "He's got a child too," she'd answered.

My mother was no longer alone. She stopped wearing kerchiefs on her head. She put blush on her cheeks. Grant did wonders for her social life. His stylish new home, good reputation, and money from the hardware store he owned brought us up in the world. In a town she'd grown up in, where everyone knew her, she was suddenly somebody.

Things had been tough for us before Grant. She never got

tired of telling me that her own parents had turned us out when she was pregnant.

"Any child conceived in a drunken stupor on Skin Island has no place in this home," my grandfather had said. Townsfolk called it "Skin Island" because it had housed a brothel in the 1940s when the pulp mill opened for business. Men came to work in Marathon from all over Canada, single men, who needed women's services. Remnants of the old building still stood on the north shore. A chunk of the door, a leg from a rusted bed frame, and a block of wood from a curlicue mirror frame were treasures amateur historians claimed and housed in the local museum.

She described the way her father had held the door open for her, his knuckles white on the doorknob, as she lugged a suitcase down the stairs. She applied for assistance and rented the row house. I barely knew my grandparents growing up. Mom kept them away from me for a long time. I'm not sure they would have come around if she hadn't. They've been coming around now that Grant and Mom are married. Grandfather has even allowed himself to be taken out for a sail by me.

"Jesse's asked for a barbecue," Grant said.

"He's been complaining about cafeteria food for nine months," I said.

"Let's surprise him with steak."

Grant tied the boat to the dock. We got in the car and drove two blocks to the town plaza. It housed Grant's hardware store, a pharmacy, a bank, and the grocery store.

Mauve petunias in stone flower pots were on sale at the garden centre. Bags of soil lined the doorway. I banged my head on a display of watering cans on the way to Grant's office. He unlocked his office door and looked over the lumber orders. He shook his head when he got to Mr. Wells' order.

"He can't pay for this. How he pays for all that whiskey, I'll never know," he said and sighed.

Wells lived in the row houses. He had three tough sons who worked after school at the pulp mill, a pregnant daughter who always smelled like boiled macaroni, and a husky dog who howled mournfully when the moon came out. I didn't know their mother. I don't know what had happened to her. Wells was always angry, yelling at his kids and kicking the dog. He once called me the spit of a drunken bull. I figured he knew, as everyone in town did, that my mother got stuck with me after getting drunk on Skin Island and spending the night in a tent with a fellow from Terrace Bay.

Grant wrote *paid in full* on the order.

"Those kids need a break."

He finished his paperwork, and we went to the grocery store. There was a sign in the window advertising watermelon. They were still available. We were lucky to get them, given how quickly the town gobbled up the seasonal fruit that was flown to Thunder Bay and then trucked three hundred kilometres down that treacherous highway to Marathon. I walked into the store and straight to the display and pulled the last melon from a sagging cardboard box. The town librarian, eight months pregnant and heaving with each step, waddled up beside me. She looked at my watermelon longingly. Mom told me that one of the pregnant women she took care of at the clinic ate a whole watermelon over the course of an afternoon. It helped to keep her feet from swelling. I looked at the librarian's feet. Her toes were puffed, waterlogged corn kernels. I didn't want to give the watermelon to her. I wanted it. I thought of Grant and his selflessness and handed it over.

At the cash register I placed the steaks on the rubber belt.

"Want my smoke break," the clerk muttered. It was Michelle O'Neill. Her black hair was lacquered with hair spray, her eyes rimmed with black kohl. She hated me. Last week, during the sewing lesson in Home Economics, she sewed the bottom of my skirt together. I got a D. Her mother never had anything nice to say to my mom either. When my mother got pregnant in grade ten, Mrs. O'Neill had called her a tramp. She was the ringleader in high school, two years older. Now she was the head nurse at the hospital where my mother worked, where she controlled the shape of my mother's days.

I handed Michelle a fifty. She slammed the till shut and placed the change on the belt. I reached to retrieve it. She put her foot on the pedal and the rubber belt screeched forward. I fumbled and missed the money.

Grant came to the till with a handful of groceries. Well aware of her games, he stared her down and she stood quiet and still.

"Jesse's favourite," he said and gestured to the barbecue sauce with bull horns on the label.

Michelle straightened out her red smock and smiled.

"Is he back for the summer?"

She turned to me and asked, as if it was totally natural for her, "Why don't you bring him to our party on Skin Island tonight?"

OVER DINNER, JESSE ASKED me about my school year. He listened as if I were the most important person at the table. I told him about the sailing club I'd started despite being mocked.

I got average grades, wasn't pretty or athletic so I didn't have much to tell him other than how fast I could change tack.

"GOOD FOR YOU," SAID Jesse.

Jesse never made me feel the way the O'Neills did. They made me feel invisible, and when they made it clear they could see me, they made me feel unworthy, a young single mother's mistake. It was easier for Jesse. Grant's wife had left him. A doting single father was tolerated. A single woman with an unplanned daughter? Harder to accept.

After dinner, Jesse presented me with a boat hook. I had a hard time docking the sailboat and this would help me reach the line. I beamed. That evening he was restless, itching for something to do. I remembered Michelle's invitation. When I mentioned it, he stood up and walked to the window. He pressed his face up against the window, pretending to survey the weather. Jesse didn't like to sail.

"You want to take the boat out to Skin Island now?"

"There's a party on the Island," I said. "I'd really like to go. I don't usually get invited. It's the in-crowd. You know them."

"You don't need them," he said with his back to me. Of course, he knew what I was up to. He always did.

"Michelle will be there."

Michelle and Jesse had dated the year before he went to college. She ditched him for one of the Wells boys the night he'd planned to take her out to the Rossport Inn for their specialty: cheesecake trifle, layered in wine glasses.

I suppose that convinced him to come to the island. He took pity on me, a shy girl with an immature longing to fit in. That's the impression he gave when he said, "Okay. Let's bust you out of that cocoon, social butterfly." But I knew part of him really wanted to see Michelle again.

Aboard the boat, he bit his bottom lip, twitched his nose every few seconds. His black hair flew from his forehead and streamed back. He was nervous, but tried not to show it.

I wanted to show him how strong my sailing skills were. I pulled the halyard for the main sail. Watched the head sail cup the wind. I changed tack deftly. It was no use. I couldn't get his attention. We docked on Skin Island and made our way across the sand toward the sheen of campfire smoke, just beyond the beach, barely into the trees.

I blushed when I saw John O'Neill. He was sitting next to his sister, the centre-of-attention, Michelle. He had the same black hair, but it curled softly around the nape of his neck. His eyes were a smoky shade of blue. His droopy mouth made him look kind. That mouth hid his true nature. He was just as harsh as anyone else in the O'Neill family. Despite what I knew my knees trembled at the sight of him.

I wanted to sit down and hike up my skirt. How could I get next to him with Michelle on one side and another girl from town on the other? Michelle rose to get Jesse a beer from the Styrofoam cooler. I quickly took her place on the dented log. My toes curled over the edge of my sandals as John's hip touched mine.

Michelle surveyed the crowd of people that had clustered around Jesse, eager to catch up, and looked for an entry point. She slid into the space to his right, vacated when one of his friends went for another round, and presented him with a beer.

As dusk drifted into night and the party slowly dissipated, the four of us were left drinking around the campfire.

"Whore Island has a great vibe after dark," John said. He winked and moved closer to me.

I giggled. He was so close I could smell tobacco on his fingertips. He placed his hand at the base of my neck. I gave a false shiver. I winced at the phoniness of feigning cold sitting next to a fire that was feasting on six-inch logs with flames as pointy as a rooster's comb. John settled in closer to me. His hands travelled up and down my back. I smiled encouragingly.

Another round of beers was offered. I'd had so much by that point I no longer cared if Jesse was about to be mangled by Michelle. All I wanted was for John to kiss me. I wasn't used to this kind of attention. Last week at school, he didn't even know I existed. I wasn't sure if he would next week. John leaned in and I got a clip of a kiss before he fell backwards off the log. Assuming it was a ploy for us to lie down; I slid off and nestled in beside him. The dry grass was sharp under my shoulder; the stars bone-white above us.

I felt pretty and sought-after, one of those girls who have boyfriends. I turned toward John expecting another kiss, but he was asleep. His mouth was open and he was drooling. Inches away from his handsome face, so close to what I'd longed for, and he'd passed out. I turned away and cursed. Of course this would happen to me. I rolled away from John and picked myself up.

I heard loud cracking noises. Michelle and Jesse were smashing their empty beer bottles against a rock. When a dozen bottles lay broken on the sand they ran hand-in-hand down the path toward the beach.

The fire had dulled. White ash covered the bright orange embers. I'd have to make sure to put out the fire. Douse the logs in water, or else it might spread. I picked up two empty bottles and walked toward the lake. I heard them before I could see them. Her coy laughter. His gentle huffs of assent. The slushing sound of water as it moved around their limbs. I turned away when her naked chest emerged from the water. She straddled his waist and swooped in for a forceful kiss.

I made my way back to the campfire empty-handed.

We should have left hours ago.

John was still asleep, cradling an empty beer bottle. I sat by myself and listened to the logs hiss. It was my fault. I shouldn't have brought Jesse here. Now that Michelle had her claws into him again, he'd inevitably get hurt. Not even Grant could tolerate her, and he had the softest heart in town.

The next morning, I woke up with John's foot under my chin. I had fallen off the log and had slept curled around his legs. My sundress was full of sand. My throat felt ashy. I was relieved that nothing had happened. I didn't know if I could bear repeating my mother's fate. She'd warned me about that her whole life.

Michelle and Jesse were coiled together. Their clothes were half-off. She woke up and brushed an unopened condom packet from her leg and threw it into the ashes.

"Tell anyone and ..."

I nodded. I wouldn't tell a soul.

She roused John, who avoided my hopeful smile, and they left in their motorboat.

Jesse woke up a while later and we made our way back to town.

"Dad's probably wondering where his boat is," he said.

"If he finds out you've been with Michelle, it's not his boat he'll be worried about."

I needn't have worried. We didn't see Michelle much after that night. She spent most of the summer at the bar with the Wells boy. Jesse called her three times, but she ignored his efforts. We didn't go back to Skin Island; the summer months moved quickly. We amused ourselves by sailing and barbecuing. At the end of August, after his last shift at the hardware store, Jesse packed his things to return to school. I drove him to the clinic the morning he was leaving to say goodbye to Mom. Michelle was sitting in the waiting room, foot tapping in agitation, trembling hand cradling her pelvis.

"I'm pregnant. It's yours. The one weekend I didn't use a condom," she said.

Jesse steered her out of the clinic, grabbed his hockey bag from the car and walked her home.

I drove home and told Grant. He got in his truck and pulled away in a hive of dust.

I felt a wave of anger at Michelle. I knew she would take everything from Jesse. And all she would do is party with the Wells boy. Michelle was like the zebra mussels that attached themselves to the bottom of our boat, she'd attach herself to a host and no one would be able to get rid of her. I wished he'd let her go. But what could I say? Jesse wouldn't listen to me. Besides, I was the one who'd wanted to go to Skin Island that night. What Jesse wanted didn't matter to me. He'd wanted to stay away from the whole lot. Why should what I want now matter to him?

I wanted him to let her raise the child alone. Let her be the brunt of ridicule. Let her live with that little cloud of shame, the one that swelled unexpectedly, and knocked the wind out of your sails and made you feel just an inch or so smaller than everyone else. I wanted her to be penetrable; I wanted some power over her.

Later that night I screamed at him, "Raise a child with her?"

"I'm not abandoning my child the way my mother did."

He sounded like he was prepared to stay with Michelle through every diaper change, tooth eruption, bump to the forehead, school day, and sick night. I left him then, no longer able to communicate without wanting to cry or hit something, and went out on the patio.

Two boats were docking on Skin Island. Behind them, in the distance, wiry Jack pine branches loomed. Sailors from all over northwestern Ontario were practicing for Grant's annual Labour Day Regatta.

Grant returned home and climbed out of his truck. He sat down and handed me the list of the regatta participants. He depended on me to organize all the entrants' information.

"Jesse will go back to college," he said.

I hoped he was right. I wanted him to get out of town, deny his husky dog nature, recalcitrant while off leash, out cavorting, only to return home, obedient, a pack animal at heart. I hoped that if Jesse left, he would be like a wolf and never want to come back home to her.

Jesse came out of the kitchen with a cup of tea for Grant.

"I've had a word with Mr. Wells. His boy will take responsibility," Grant said.

"I can't do that, Dad. I don't want my child to —"

"Be raised by a stepfather?" I said.

"No one's going to know the child is yours. And they'll never want for anything," Grant said.

The next morning, Jesse was standing beside the bus, waiting to board it to leave for school. Not too far off, Michelle, parked in her car, called Jesse to her. I could see her looking at him imploringly.

He hung his head.

I trembled, afraid of what she was probably saying. But the weight of what was within her thickening belly had dulled her hostility. She simply swore. Her words pierced Jesse's indifference. His face churned with grief and shame and sadness. When he stepped on that bus, it was the last time he set foot in Marathon.

"PUT MY ASHES IN a bottle and throw me in the lake," Grant had said when I'd asked him how he wanted to be buried. His cancer came quickly that spring and deflated the wind from his sails within a month. I went with him to the clinic every day and Mom would play cards with us on her lunch breaks. Despite everything, we laughed and carried on like life was limitless.

He was hopeful, spent the last year of life — the year they tore the pulp mill smokestack down, after all the gold had been extracted and the mining families had left — raising funds to clear and revitalize what he called the Group of Seven Lake Superior Trail in the hopes of attracting tourists to town. Uncertain about their future, town councillors and local teachers hoped to trade on the scenic views and walking tours through a landscape that had mesmerized the world, immortalized through early-twentieth-century paintings, for sustenance. Once again relying on trees, rock, and water to procure necessities.

After securing a hefty grant from the bank, right after the May long weekend, Grant died. We threw the bottle filled with his ashes in the cove and watched as it lay immobile in the harbour, seemingly moored in a flat lake with no wind or current.

"This is ridiculous," Mom said and waded in waist deep water to retrieve the wine bottle. She refused to throw him out as he'd wished and kept him perched on her windowsill.

THE SUN DUCKED BEHIND the hem of an oblong cloud. A few sailboats docked in the harbour. The young sailor came up the hill, black hair flattened by the wind. Up close I could see the impish nose, wide smile, and thumb-deep indent in his chin he shared with his grandfather. Easy to see he'd inherited a passion for sailing. I wondered if he'd been practicing for the regatta. He'd be old enough now, surely, to participate. I hoped he wouldn't. I didn't want to see him. He didn't know me, but I knew he lived in a row house with his mother Michelle and the Wells boy, who was and wasn't a boy anymore. She still works at the grocery store, but is taking a college math course. Mom told me she solves algebraic equations between customers at the till.

As I curled up in the blanket, I felt ashamed of my resentment toward this boy, who took my brother away, whose presence reminded me of the time we'd lost the only father I'd known. I couldn't help but feel that the island turned me into what I'd hated most: someone who sneered at a child who didn't — and wouldn't ever — know his own father. And the smug pride I took in knowing that it wasn't me who got pregnant after drinking all night on Skin Island. Easier to blame that island. The curse of its history, the way it played a role in shaping our lives. Because I knew that people like Mrs. O'Neill, and my grandparents, would never change, even if it concerned their own flesh and blood. And kids from shamed mothers are vulnerable to their disdain no matter the good grades we get, the careers we build, or the families we go on to create.

# Lake Effect

IT'S A SIGN, FIORELLA thinks; he's been living in Saint-Joseph-de-Beauce, Québec for nine years while we were in Saint Joseph, Michigan. It's a sign. *Santos* — his last name — means Saints in Italian. Not one Saint, but two osr more. She'd been studying, looking up Italian words, in case he still spoke the language he used when she was a kid A language of songs about saints and villagers and the drowning of a contrary wife.

Sitting on her hands for twenty minutes, waiting for the bus to move, determined not to bite her nails, she needed to know, now that she was eighteen, where her father was. She remembered a man with black hair, scruffy beard, hairy knuckles, and a belt clinched tightly around waist.

And the letter he'd sent all those years ago, said a cousin who'd married a French Canadian needed help with his restaurant. He still loved them both. He'd send what he could.

Fio wanted to change seats, but the driver in the aisle, polyester slacks smelling like mushrooms, stooped over to check her ticket and blocked her way. Without momentum as a distraction — roadside scenery, road signs, speed limits — there was no way to avoid thoughts of her mother, Sandy, and their confrontation last night.

"You've had his address all this time?"

"I didn't want him to hurt you. He left us. Me. You."

Fio called her mother a cunt. *A cunt.*

Sandy called one of the men she played pool with. He came to get her. They stayed out all night and came home the next morning. Her hair was in knots, her mascara had bled down her cheeks, and she was still drunk.

Fio stayed by herself, practiced ballet in her room for hours. She'd turned off her computer, now that she knew where to find him. Over the years she'd been on Facebook, Google, Instagram: nothing. And all that time her mother knew where he was. She wanted to find him so she could spit at him. Cuddle and laugh with him. She wanted to show him her dancing, and have him marvel at her growth, and talent, and treat her presence as if it were a precious gift, a child's crude finger painting placed on the refrigerator, faultless. She wanted him to be proud of her. She wanted to be his again — his child, his darling. She wanted his love.

She wanted to kick him.

How dare he leave? How dare he leave her and her mother to fend for themselves.

No more wistful dreaming or trying to hold onto images that drifted in and out of memory. He was real. Alive. Grown older over the years, but alive. Was she like him? Did they look alike? Could she blame him for her hairy upper lip? Or the crooked incisor on the left side of her mouth? She could remember his laugh, could hear it sometimes in her own. If she remembered a jovial man who laughed a lot, where did the unhappiness come from that made him leave?

The bus pulled out. Fio slept until it stopped in Detroit. Fio stepped out, amid a flurry of other passengers, rolling suitcases, a crowd of smokers satiating their cravings, lighting up, thin cylinders of white paper sizzling in the sun. She found the express bus service to the airport. She boarded a plane to Québec City.

Two hours later, she was passing through Canadian customs. She noticed all the signage was in French. Did he speak French? How did she expect to make her way around when she didn't even speak French?

IN QUÉBEC CITY, WAITING for the connecting bus, bright blue and white streamers, plump balloons and handmade signs everywhere, Fiorella couldn't understand a word. The bus was late, due to the Saint-Jean-Baptiste Day Parade. A woman in a navy uniform announced, first in French and then in English, that sandwiches and juice would be provided while they waited. Impatient, Fiorella sat down, weak-kneed and exhausted from travelling. She didn't want to arrive in St. Joseph's at night; she didn't want to skulk around his house after dark. She wanted to be there in time for supper, to see if he would recognize her right away.

"*Ça va?*" the woman in the navy uniform asked gently, "Are you hungry? Your knees are shaking."

Fio looked up at her, "No, I'm fine."

"Where are you going?"

"To Saint-Joseph-de-Beauce."

"Ah, *oui*, yes, that bus is here, on platform *deux*, two, you are here in three, see?"

She got up and walked towards the bus, boarded it, jostled for a seat, collapsed into it, nausea rising as the idling bus lurched into gear. No one around her spoke English. Nothing made sense. She wasn't sure how long the trip would be, but was relieved to see the road sign for Saint-Joseph-de-Beauce within an hour. She'd booked a room online at the Gite L'Aubergine, a modest bed and breakfast, painted a garish pink and yellow. All she wanted was one night. One night, that's it. Her one chance to see him before her life changed and she moved to New York City.

AT THE INN, A young black-haired man named Stéphane, a smear of acne on his cheek, showed her to a room. He spoke English. There isn't much to do, he said, but the Saint-Jean-Baptiste parade is marching toward the church. There's a barbecue. If she wanted to get out and have supper he would walk her there, his shift had just ended.

"No, I want to go to the Italian restaurant."

"It's closed. Everything is. But they always have a booth at the barbecue."

SHE EMERGED FROM HER room, freshly showered, wearing a white cotton dress, hair knotted in a high bun. He smiled at her and they walked up the main street of the small town.

"How was your trip?"

"What?" she said, numb with anxiety.

At the church, fiddle music filled the air. Through the thick crowd of townspeople, she suddenly saw him. Her father. A short Italian man with her eyebrows and wide cheeks. She stepped forward, opening her mouth to call to him, but before the word left her mouth, she heard "Papa!" from a small girl in a yellow dress.

Fio's father stopped, turned around, to the direction the young voice had come from. He squatted and held out his arms for the child. He hoisted her up with his left arm. She curled into his chest. A pretty, thin woman, in a mid-length, pink floral dress, walked toward him and ruffled the child's hair.

They spoke in French. The crowd swelled and swallowed the family.

Fio frowned. She was frustrated she could no longer see her father. Her sister. She didn't want to see them enough to wade through the crowd, but she didn't want to lose sight of them so immediately.

The trill of singers' voices hovered above the ambient noise of the evening. It was late in the day, but the sun was still bright and well above the horizon. It was just after the solstice and she was farther north than St. Joseph, Michigan. The shadows were growing longer and they swallowed the crowd that had swelled around him. He was gone. Fio calmed her breathing and strode purposefully towards the booth of the Italian restaurant. She scanned every pair of blue eyes, every shock of black hair, until she found him sitting at a picnic table, a bottle of beer in front, his wife beside and the child on his lap.

Fio dodged his eyes, slunk behind a canopy as Stéphane went to get them beers in red plastic cups. She stood behind the tent and peeped around it at her father. He was eating a hamburger, joking with a man seated across from him, nuzzling his wife. She crossed her arms to give her a better sense of being centered. She rubbed her elbows and focused on the feel of the skin under her fingertips: rough, dry, stretched over hard bone, movable cartilage. Tactile things she trusted. But her legs were letting her down. She wanted to leave, get away from what she saw, but they wouldn't move. Stéphane arrived. "Drink?" She didn't answer him. Her father was arm wrestling the man at his picnic table. After a respectable minute, he flattened the fellow's forearm to the wood. "You are shaking," she heard Stéphane say. "What's wrong?"

HOW MUCH HAD SHE drunk? She'd lost track after the first bottle of wine. Stéphane stayed up with her, awake until four, maybe five. She hadn't checked after the last time she looked at her cellphone. That had been at three-thirty, a minute before Stéphane uncorked what she remembered as the last bottle of wine. The one that did the trick and blotted out the image of the happy family she wasn't a part of.

As for her newfound friend Stéphane, she couldn't get enough of him; silly, witty, verbose Stéphane, who regaled her with stories of guests until they fell asleep on the floor. The man from Montreal who took his wife and mistress to the Gîte l'Aubergine for the weekend, kept them on separate floors, and his wife was none the wiser. Fio had laughed at his stories, but not the monotony of his life: cooking, cleaning, updating social media, posting guests' photos, living in isolation in a small apartment at the back of the house, off the kitchen, with his parents.

The time with Stéphane last night had kept the shock of seeing her father with his new family from eating away at her. But the gnawing had returned this morning. And such pain was always sharper the morning after a binge.

She'd have to get up. The sunlight pulsed through the slats on the blinds. She couldn't smell breakfast, so she figured she'd missed it. Ashamed for wasting her morning in bed, when she could be — what? — enjoying early morning espressos and reminiscing about good times with Pops and family?

What the fuck was she supposed to do now? Call him up? Surprise him at his restaurant? Yes. That's what she'd do. Were they open for lunch? Stéphane would know. He'd bring her there if she asked. Of course he would. She wouldn't have to go it alone.

"You'll have to go alone," Stéphane said. "It's already past two." He had rooms to clean. He offered his car, the walk to the Italian Restaurant was up hill and would take fifteen minutes, but the drive would take less than five.

Behind the wheel of his Honda Civic, she composed herself. Dizzy and dehydrated, she adjusted the seat and the rear-view mirror. Her eyes were bloodshot and she looked weary. She started the car and pulled out and drove, following Stéphane's simple directions. She saw a small white tower, resembling a gazebo, jutting from a modest white building. She slowed, pulled over, and parked in front of the restaurant. Two lattice pillars with plastic flowers entwined supported a red-and-white canopy over the entrance. A sign in the window, backed by lace curtains, read *Open*.

Her cellphone buzzed. Her mother. Five messages already warning her about him, telling her to drop it, leave it, come home, she loved her — all riddled with typos, indications of her aversion to texting. Fio turned the phone off and left it in the car before she made her way to the front door. She opened the door slowly and stepped inside. A chime sounded, alerting the staff they had customers. The room smelled like candle wax, onions, and baked bread. The space was sparsely decorated. Bare wooden tables, a long bar at the side of the room, ceiling fans on slow speed. The woman Fio had seen yesterday — dark hair curling over her shoulders, red lipstick like a strip of paint from a fire engine, and blue eyes flecked with yellow like forget-me-nots — smiled and shepherded her to a seat. Warmer, prettier, healthier than Mom. No wonder.

The menu was red-sauce Italian. It was lunchtime and she didn't feel like heavy pasta on her stomach. They had soup. "Minestrone?" she blurted. The woman nodded and turned around, heading for the kitchen.

FIO SEARCHED THE WOMAN'S face as she placed a bowl of soup, bread and cheese, and mineral water before her. She watched her move around the room, as familiar with the mechanics of the restaurant as if it were an extension of her body, full of the certainty that comes from working here day in and day out.

The minestrone was actually very good. She found herself enjoying it — to the point of almost forgetting her hangover and her reason for being in Saint-Joseph-de-Beauce. The door opened and he backed his way in, a case of wine in his arms. He headed straight to the bar, stopping to kiss his wife quickly on the cheek. As he opened the box and pulled the bottles out, Fio wrapped her arms around herself. She didn't know where to look. She moved the peony in the vase and pretended that she could actually hide behind it. She caught snatches of their conversation. She wasn't sure if they were speaking French or Italian. Both sounded the same to her. She thought she heard the word "artiste." Was his wife an artist?

Fio peeped out from behind the flower. Her father's eyes met hers.

He was handsome, dark wavy hair slicked back, a streak of grey starting at his widow's peak. His eyes, a marbled blue, widened as he looked at her. He stopped talking and unpacking the wine bottles and tilted his head.

The chime above the door jangled and an elderly couple entered. His wife greeted them and gestured to a table near the window. Fio looked up to see her father standing in front of her.

"Fio?"

He gently nudged the peony aside.

Her throat constricted and her vocal cords were useless. She put down her spoon, her hand had begun to shake. It must have been a jolt of adrenalin from hearing him speak. Or was it cortisol? One was for fear, the other stress. What was she feeling? Up close, memories of him, pieces of the puzzle in her mind, matched the man in front of her. Coconut-scented pomade, hair on his arms, black and thick, curling under the sleeves of his white chef's coat.

He was speaking accented English to her. "My love, is it really you? What are you — how did you get here?" He sat and reached for her hand, letting go quickly when her nose wrinkled at his touch. His face contorted slightly. Fio wondered if untamed thoughts were racing through his mind; did he want to verbalize them? His lips pursed. He raised his hands. Was he about to say more? No. He had asked his questions.

"Hello," she said.

Hands on the table, he relaxed.

"You're what? Eighteen now. Is your mother here too?"

Fio looked down at her soup bowl. Pasta and tomatoes and spinach. She shook her head no, and looked up to say the word, but her father had started to speak.

"Fiorella, my wife Micheline." Her father indicated the woman now standing beside him.

Fio smiled weakly and Micheline leaned in and kissed her on both cheeks.

"It is a pleasure to meet you," Micheline said.

"I have something to tell you," he said.

Fio toyed with her soup spoon for a moment, waiting to hear her father who abandoned her say aloud what she saw for herself the day before.

"I have a daughter."

"I know. I saw you at the festival yesterday."

"Why didn't you — Where are you staying?"

Fio didn't know how to respond to her father. Did he really not understand why she did not interrupt the happy family she saw yesterday? Was he really about to suggest that she come to stay with them?

"How long are you here?"

She couldn't answer.

"You can stay with us. You can get to know your sister."

Sister, thought Fio. Sister.

"I'm going to pick her up from school soon. Do you want to come?"

"No, no," Micheline said quickly. "I'll go. You stay. Of course you stay." She turned to Fio. "Will you stay for supper?"

Bewildered, Fio nodded. What exactly was the plan? Her father got up, as if realizing where he was and that he had a job to do. He went to tend to the elderly couple, the only patrons in the restaurant. Fio looked at the empty seat in front of her, at all the empty seats, and wanted to hide. There weren't enough peonies in the place to camouflage the flush of pink flooding her cheeks.

She was ashamed that she'd come. Embarrassed. Micheline would soon be home from school with their daughter, and they'd behave like a family. A regular family with its own rituals. How was school? Did you eat all of your lunch? Do you have homework? Would you like meatloaf for dinner? Or would her sister be able to request anything from the menu for dinner every night?

What was Fio to do in the midst of all this ordinary domesticity, interrupt and yell, By the way, I'm your sister? She pushed the thought out of her mind. She didn't come here to be a sister, to play that role. She came to be his daughter, to be with him, not to share him.

Two young girls came out of the kitchen in black uniforms to orchestrate seating and service. Her father went in the kitchen. Fio sat alone.

"*Plus de soupe?*"

"Huh?" she said.

"More soup?" the waitress asked.

She shook her head no. She looked around for her father. She couldn't see him. That's all that's in the offing? Disappointment took hold. The muscles in her abdomen seized, pinched both sides of her ribs, butterfly wings retreating back into a hardened and discarded cocoon, re-wrapping itself in the hopes of disappearing. That's what she'd do — disappear — slip quietly from her seat. Get back in Stéphane's car. Wake up tomorrow and go back home.

She pushed back her chair just as Micheline returned with the girl in her arms. It was like looking at a childhood picture of herself. They shared the same hair colour. The girl had Fiorella's — her father's — eyes, nose, and skin. The only difference was the child had Micheline's lips. An unexpected warmth, a peony-sized bloom of love. What a cute, tiny thing. She didn't want to leave; she wanted to hold her. She didn't know the child, but wanted to get to know her. And then her feelings froze. A sudden iceberg. How could he have left Fio when she was just like that, so tiny, vulnerable, cute. Loveable. She started to head for the door.

Micheline saw her and rushed over.

"Don't go, we can take tomorrow off, come by for lunch," Micheline said and pulled a pencil crayon from the child's backpack and scribbled an address on a napkin.

"Aggie, say hello to Fiorella."

Fio took the napkin. She hurried out the door, walked to the

Honda Civic, got in; and in the rear-view mirror, her father standing by the window holding his daughter, watching her go.

"NEW YORK?"

Fio nodded. Baked beans, a meat pie, and a slice of bread before her.

"I should have known you'd become a dancer. I met your mother in a Detroit nightclub and she could shake —"

"Tea?" Micheline asked.

Fio asked for a coffee instead and cursed Micheline for interrupting. She wanted to hear about her mother and father.

"I used to go to New York City when I was a kid. My aunt — your great-aunt, well both of you," he said and gestured to Aggie, "— lived in Brooklyn."

Aggie pouted when Micheline placed a piece of toast on her plate.

"It's burned," he said and scraped it. "How do you like yours?"

"Lightly toasted with butter," Fio answered.

Micheline placed two cups of tea on the table, a plastic cup for Aggie, and another for Fio. Fio looked at the wilted square of paper dangling on the side of the cup. Fio hated tea.

"Aggie loves her milky tea," he said. "She takes after Micheline. Your mother and I loved our coffee. Oh, you wanted coffee? Micheline?"

"Sorry," Micheline said and got up to pour a cup. "I was thinking you both might like to go for a bike ride after lunch? Show her the sights?"

Fio smiled. Alone time with him. At last.

Pedaling behind him, in a borrowed pair of Micheline's shoes, two sizes too big, Fio watched the muscles in his tanned arms clench and ripple, undulate throughout his back. In a white tank top, he had the body of a thirty-year-old. In all the time he'd been gone, her mother's body had suffered, ravaged by drink and loneliness. But he'd kept his shape. Pretty clear who the injured party was.

They cycled along the Chaudière River. Her father pointed out a National Historic Site and they stopped to marvel at l'Église Saint-Joseph and the cluster of buildings beside it: the convent, presbytery, orphanage, and the Lambert School. "Classical Revival style," he said. "Micheline is working on her art history degree online so I'm learning too."

Soft green hills behind the church's white spire; the convent's steep pyramidal roof; the presbytery with gables, dormers, and tall chimneys; the orphanage with its projecting frontispiece and mansard roof; and the Lambert School with its large, monumental, three-storey massing were impressive.

They stopped for another cup of coffee at a tiny café.

"When does school start?"

"August."

"How's Sandy?" Joey asked.

Fio wasn't sure what to say. This was the first time he'd asked about her mother.

"Lonely."

Joey looked away.

Should she ask him why he left? Would they have that moment, right here, sitting in this café? It was the reason she came. She came to confront him. But no. Seeing him was enough for now. The fact that he didn't know her — and the impact of knowing that — was bigger than any rationale he could give her for leaving them fifteen years ago. Sure, he could tell her why, but it wouldn't change the fact that he knew how Aggie liked her toast, and hadn't a clue how she liked hers.

Joey pulled something out of his pocket.

"My mother gave me this St. Joseph medallion when I was leaving upstate New York to come and live with your mother. He's the patron saint of travellers and fathers."

He pressed the silver medallion into her hand.

She didn't need a patron saint. Especially one of fathers. She wanted a father. She needed to know him, this man, this stranger, who sat before her and grappled with his past.

"Back then," he said, and she cringed.

They were going to have that moment.

He told her things she already knew. That he'd left four brothers and Catholic parents behind in Syracuse, New York to wash dishes at an uncle's restaurant in Detroit, when he'd met her mother at a nightclub.

He told her things she didn't know. That Sandy had been between men, no, literally, gyrating on the dance floor between two auto workers when she spotted Joey and made her way over. She left with him. Persuaded him to come to St. Joseph when she found out she was pregnant. Told him he could work at her father's charter fishing company. He'd have done anything for her. While she did anyone, anywhere, all the time. He'd caught her a few times, on her father's boat, in the backseat of his car, behind the hot dog stand at the beach, but he'd forgive her quickly. She always promised to stop.

Sandy could do no wrong. She was her father's pride and joy. Her father, Bill, had come to St. Joseph in 1973 from Flint, a disgruntled auto factory worker, during the oil crisis. He'd grown up there, his father employed at the GM factory, a satisfied family man raising kids at the height of the fifties' prosperity. But Sandy's father, like Sandy herself, was never satisfied. The wind called him west, the screech of gulls a piper's tune, beckoned him to the water. At thirty years old, unmarried, unhappy, sweating it out on the assembly line, he cashed his last paycheque, closed his bank account, skipped out on last month's rent and made for the tiny town of Saint Joseph — a town riddled with economic uncertainty itself — where the abandoned waterfront, with aching memories of once-popular carousels and go-karts, looked to him like a gold coast waiting to be plundered.

He got a small business loan and bought himself a twenty-one-foot heated and enclosed river boat and set up charter fishing expeditions along the river to catch bass, catfish, suckers, walleye, and sheephead. Once he'd made a little bit of money — saving on rent by living on the boat itself, with just the fish he caught to eat — he bought himself a thirty-foot charter and offered excursions on the lake to wrangle perch from June to August and salmon and trout from early spring until September.

By the time the Laboratory Equipment Corporation bought and cleaned up Silver Beach, his business was established. People from all over Michigan flocked to the locale; charter fishing was the thing to do. He bought a small bungalow for his young wife, set up a swing-set in the backyard for his daughter Sandy, named after the honey-coloured beaches.

Fio was five when Grandpa Bill took out a charter and never returned. Seven miles offshore, a wave capsized the boat. Joey and the fishermen were rescued and treated for hypothermia. Bill, who never wore a lifejacket, hit his head in the accident and drowned.

Sandy's behaviour worsened after her father died. She drank and it didn't matter who she went home with.

"I couldn't take it anymore. I loved her, but she didn't love me enough to stop. I told her I was leaving and taking you with me. She said she'd kill me if I tried."

"Mom's been lying to me all these years?"

"Sin of omission," said her father.

Silly foolish girl I am, thinking the men came after he left. The men she drank and played pool with. The men she stayed out all night with. A memory came then of the day they moved in with her grandmother. When she was ten, Sandy took her down to the waterfront and walked along the beach barefoot, hand in hand. Sandy sang "With or Without You". The singing soothed Fio and made her feel comforted, but Sandy sang louder whenever dark-haired men walked by. It was mortifying, her mother trying to get the attention of handsome swarthy men. They stopped at a food stand and Sandy complained about her waistline all the way home after she sucked the skin off a fried chicken leg.

"There's more. I had a breakdown. I survived and your Grandpa didn't. He thought he was invincible, but I was and it tore me up when he died. He left the business to me. I was to fill out insurance forms, get a new fleet, and get back on the water and provide for my family. Only I couldn't get back on the water. I couldn't go near the water. And I couldn't face you or your mother when I felt like a coward. So I left without any fight."

Fio tried to ignore the image in her mind, the one that had haunted her since childhood. The one where Grandpa fell unconscious beneath the seamless amplitude of the waves, swallowing him in one gulp.

"I can't change the past, but we can have a future," her father said.

She swallowed her coffee. Enough bad memories. She wanted to remember the good things.

"Will you speak to me in Italian?"

"*Un uomo, la cui moglie era annegato in un torrente.*"

She closed her eyes as he spoke. She remembered this fable. He was telling her the story of a man whose wife had drowned and how he went up the river to look for the body. A young boy advised him to follow the flow of the current. In that case, said the man, I won't find her. When she was alive, she was contrary and went against the ways of others; now that she is dead, she will go against the current.

She thought of the last time she heard it. The winter after Grandpa drowned. He took her to North Pier after the lake-effect snow storm. They walked through town, half-buried in snow, toward the beach to get to the frozen lake. He carried her over boulders of ice just to stand near the tip of the lighthouse. Icicles covered the tower and walkway. Frozen water in mid-wave covered half the tower, the lantern room, and muted the light. It coated the bridge with a frozen skin higher than a sand dune. It was beautiful, worth the trip, but he'd hurried them home afterward, fearful of frostbite, the type you could get in those parts that left ice crystals in your feet.

After reciting the fable, he told her that you can't change people no matter how hard you try. Any more than you can change a wave bound for shore. She should have known then what he was trying to tell her. But she didn't. Hadn't a clue. How could she have known?

Family responsibilities were contrary to Sandy's nature. She was, is, and would always prefer a party girl's life. She was never a family woman like she was supposed to be; that was going against the current.

"*Plus de café?*" the waiter asked.

"*Non, merci,*" her father said.

Her eyes moistened with the first pull of a teardrop. The stories brought back too many memories. Her emotions felt like correspondence that she'd successfully kept private for years, but now the envelope had been steamed open, and the sordid contents were on display. She didn't know what else to say. They sat across from one another in a comfortable silence.

THE PORT AUTHORITY BUS terminal in New York City was crowded with people of all kinds dragging loud black suitcases on weak wheels. Fio, clad in sweater, scarf, and baby-blue leotard underneath a wool skirt, stood on the arrivals platform waiting for a bus, late from Montreal. Stéphane was coming to visit. They'd been emailing and Skyping.

Her lower back ached. She'd slipped in rehearsals for La Sylphide, falling on a stage prop, bumping her tailbone. Her classmates asked about the bruise daily.

The bus finally pulled in. The door opened and she saw his black hair first, then the slope of his lean shoulder. His blue eyes stood out in the sepia crowd. He waved and hurried towards her. A smile buoyed her cheeks, "Stéphane!"

The last time she'd seen him, after cycling with her father that afternoon, she returned to the inn and packed her things. Burst into tears when Stéphane asked her if she wanted supper. Told him why she'd come and why she wanted to leave. She didn't know her own mother or father, she said and sobbed. She's untrustworthy and he's no more than a stranger.

Stéphane opened a bottle of wine. He poured two glasses and they talked. She wondered if he would make a move. When he was opening the second bottle, he blurted out that he wanted to visit New York City so he could go to a gay club.

Walking from the bus terminal — Stéphane agog at the crowds of people and the lights and buildings towering above — she thought of her first weekend in New York. She'd flown to the city after a long summer working at St. Joseph's final Venetian Festival, a boating, arts, and music extravaganza. After thirty-three years it had grown too large and loud for the community and so the small arts festival — once confined to the arboretum, a place where decades of tree growth ejected the festival onto the streets — was finally put to bed by citizens unwilling to handle the traffic, congestion, and crowds.

She'd avoided her mother all summer through work. A few times Fio had hinted at what she knew, but her angry mother avoided any discussion. Fio sneered at her as if she were a child. She was childlike. Irresponsible. A woman who'd never tell the truth. No way to get her to admit. When she left, that final night, her mother in a robe, having come downstairs from entertaining a fellow, Fio told her quite plainly that she knew.

"What do you know? Nothing. Nothing wrong with how I live my life," her mother said.

"Don't know when I'll be back," Fio said.

Audible relief in Sandy's sigh coupled with a muffled cough from upstairs.

There were numerous emails from Quebec, full of photos, a stiff-looking Fio standing on the doorstep of his house, on the eve of her departure, and scenes from the ensuing summer: Aggie at the carnival, Aggie in the kitchen with her father, Aggie cycling with him. And his personal messages, *so glad you came, would like to visit, come visit next spring, how's your Mother?* Fio slowly, begrudgingly — ashamed of herself, her weakness, her neediness, and everything that was wrapped up in a silly sense of hope of knowing him finally — looked forward to their correspondences.

Alone that first day in New York City, Fio had walked these same streets. Amidst a street food festival near Washington Square Park, the heat and steam and the smell of corn and churros rising in tufts, drifting over lower Manhattan. She walked down to Battery Park, where thousands had gathered to celebrate the unveiling of a statue celebrating Mother Teresa's canonization, and wandered through streets swelling with jazzy street noise bordered by immense buildings. One glimpse of the Statue of Liberty in the harbour and she knew that this was the place she would blossom in, find her footing and stand as triumphant as the statue, enjoy freedom from family, and live her life in full, detach from her mother, leave her to the life she wanted.

Her father had sent her an espresso maker. She placed it on her windowsill in the dorm room shared with a girl from Detroit. She was happy that he had thought of her, touched by the gift. She was nervous, but looked forward to seeing him and Micheline and Aggie next summer. When they told Aggie on Skype that Fiorella was her sister she reached out and tried to touch her. She begged Fio to come back. Fio felt awkward, but smiled.

"Hungry?" Fiorella asked as they approached the Second Street Residence.

Stéphane nodded.

"East Village? Big Gay Ice Cream?"

# Shoreline

SHE CAN'T LET THEM take him. The room has everything he needs. A wall-mounted bookshelf with plenty of picture books. A dresser cluttered with creams and powders, and inside the drawers, sweaters and pants and shirts and shoes. Crib with yellow bedspread against one wall, her bed against the other. Most infants sleep in the same room as their mothers, sometimes in the same bed, but not here. Babies are not allowed to co-sleep. They have to go back into their cribs.

Her things are kept to one drawer, a few polycotton T-shirts, two pairs of khakis and six white socks, a bra with a hole for nursing. No one is allowed to keep razors.

What bothers all the women most is the smell of industrial cleaner. The mop comes out once they are safely in their cells. Doors locked behind them, like dogs in kennels. Blinds, which must be closed every evening, hide the rusted bars. It's quiet; the only noise in this wing is the prison guard's ringtone, the keyboard solo from Van Halen's *Jump*.

Her son Ashton, asleep in his crib, breath snagging on dry snot, more at peace here in this prison in Decatur than she ever was back home in Wheaton, Illinois. Even though he is happy, she might lose him. The governor wants to shut down Decatur's Moms and Babies program on the grounds that her son, and others like him, shouldn't be raised by women behind bars.

This afternoon the decision will be announced.

IT WAS LATE AFTERNOON when they found her, lying on North Avenue Beach in Chicago. Lake water ebbed and flowed around her head, carrying her hair up and down. She spat at the officers when they picked her up and took her away. Hours later, she awoke in a windowless cell that smelled like wet dog fur. She tried to move, but couldn't; it felt like ants were crawling under her skin.

"Help."

"Water and crackers," said an overweight prison guard.

"I can't sit up."

The guard sat her up and put the cup of water to her mouth. She swallowed and then threw up. The guard eased her back down and locked the cell.

They asked for her name.

"Fuck you."

"If you don't tell us your name, we'll put you in solitary confinement," the officer said.

She sneered. Fought them at every turn. Wouldn't eat and wouldn't answer questions. She bit a prison guard's finger.

They took her to the doctor after she'd pulled clumps of hair out by the handful.

"You're almost two months pregnant. We can give you methadone," the doctor said.

The overweight prison guard escorted her back to her cell. She met the guard's big brown eyes and clutched her arm tightly, allowed the guard to gently wipe hair away from her face.

When she told them her name, she cried and begged them not to take her back home.

"You don't have to go home. You're an adult," the officer said.

"What month is it?" she asked.

"October."

Five months ago she'd turned eighteen.

"But you're facing criminal charges," he said. "You're not going home yet."

SHE'D GROWN UP IN Wheaton. In a fancy house in a desirable neighbourhood. Professionals ran the place: landscapers, cleaning staff, a part-time cook. Mother practiced family law. Father presided in criminal court, often criticized by the Republican media for being too lenient, sentences half of what they should be, sentencing via community work instead of jail time. His adversaries invariably predicted that most criminals who found themselves in Judge Wise's court were sure to reoffend.

She wished her father had been lenient with her. Or giving. Loving. Her mother, less emotionally stingy. Both of them, away, working all the time. She'd been lonely. Tired of talking to herself, watching, listening, swiping, clicking. Online, every day after school and on weekends, alone. Too timid to join teams, or practice an art.

SHE MET ASHTON'S FATHER, Lachlan, almost three years ago. She was sixteen. He was twenty. At North Avenue Beach with her friend Isabel, burying themselves in sand and sculpting mermaid's tales when he scuttled over.

He wore a White Sox cap backwards, visor stiff as a plank.

He was shirtless, hairless, and had a six-pack. A sterling silver skull-and-cross-bones charm hung from his pierced belly button. It jingled against his white boxer shorts that bulged out of denim cut-offs.

She was up to her neck in sand when he offered her tart lemonade from the tip of a lime green plastic straw. He looked at her like she was perfect.

"What are you called, Dakota or Mackenzie?" he asked.

"Madeline," she said.

"You want to ditch this suburb-nerd-herd and come downtown?" he'd asked.

"My parents are here."

"Next weekend?"

NEXT SATURDAY SHE TOLD her parents she'd booked a study room at the Harold Washington Library. She met Lachlan at a restaurant around the corner. He ordered a triple-patty hamburger, dripping with cheese, soft egg yolk and mashed avocado. They shared a basket of fries.

"What does your Father do?" she asked.

"Construction," Lachlan said.

He winked and told a joke, "I didn't believe my Dad was stealing from the highway road crew, until I got home and all the signs were there."

She smiled. Bit a crispy fry in half and thought *He'll have to do much better than that.*

He told her another one, "How do construction workers party? They raise the roof."

Despite herself, she laughed. A few hours later, giddy from stupid fun, he pulled a joint from a pocket he'd sewn on the inside of his ball cap.

"Mind if I smoke this?"

"Of course not," she'd said, pretending she smoked too. Her first puff was clumsy, but the effect it had on her was wonderful. She loved it. It took the edge off. Walking back to the train she wanted to kiss him, but he stroked her nose and said he'd text.

On their next date they walked along the canal, watched city lights at sunset, ate deep dish pizza, and smoked until they laughed themselves silly. She accidentally ate the paper on her ice cream cone. He kept tripping over the cuffs on his jeans.

When school finished the following week, she was supposed to go to her Grandmother's house in Yellow Springs, Ohio, as usual, but the thought of another long, lonely summer forced her hand.

She packed a bag and boarded the train to Chicago. As the train picked up speed she wondered if she was doing the right thing. If they found her, they'd kill her for making them worry, for letting Grandma down. But the thought of not seeing Lachlan for the summer was unimaginable. She turned away from the window and put her hood up.

The house in Englewood was not what she'd expected. The walls were streaked with water stains. Mold spotted the ceiling, the floors were warped, window frames were rotten and smears of mud covered the panes of glass. That first night she woke up to the sound of gunfire. Cuddled into Lachlan, she wondered if she'd made a mistake. He held her and stroked her hair. "This neighbourhood is crazy, but I'll protect you. I promise," he said.

The next morning Lachlan had left a pot of tea on the bedside table and a note; he'd gone to work at a site with his father and would be home at six. His housemates had stayed out late, but now they were home: two of them lying in the doorway, one slumped over the kitchen table, and another tucked into a corner. Red flea-bite-sized marks on their arms, needles on the kitchen table.

She collected up the things she'd come with, threw them in her backpack and, stifling the urge to vomit as she crept over the two passed out by the door, left the apartment and ran to the nearest bus stop. She caught the 63 Red Line and rode it to North Avenue Beach.

She removed her sneakers, tied the laces together, and slung them through the straps on her backpack. She waded into the lake, calf-deep. The sailboats appeared to be cushioned by the swath of sparkling blue water. She yearned for the comfort of home. Turning back to the beach, she saw anxious faces jutting forward, sniffer dogs yanking on their leashes.

"Maddie, love, where have you been?"

She ran toward them. She felt overwhelmingly guilty and blurted out, "Mom, Dad, I'm sorry, I met a guy and stayed at his place."

"NICE PLACE," SAID LACHLAN, and not much else for the rest of the evening.

Dinner consisted of a Thai bowl, made by her mother. Her father bought Jones Soda, but took out cans of beer when he saw Lachlan.

That night, Madeline's mother wept. Her father held her. She knew what her daughter saw in Lachlan. He *saw* her. Every word, glimpse, gesture spoke of his strong feelings. Her mother wouldn't admit it was love. This young man thought he was in love with their only child, when he only lusted after her. To make it worse, she knew Madeline felt the same way. Lonely, impressionable Madeline was a follower, she did what her friends wanted just so that she would belong somewhere, anywhere.

"Do you think he'll hurt her?" her mother asked. She pictured a pregnancy, a baby, Lachlan's certain absence. She knew it was already too late to talk to Madeline; any discussion with her parents would only give him the advantage.

One of them should have stayed home, to guide and love and support. One of them should have. But no, that was a faulty argument. Her friend Isabel, who also had two working parents, had attracted no such character. She was left alone too, fended for herself in a house with a nanny and a housekeeper.

In the morning, her parents had left for Ohio before Madeline awoke. Neither of them wanted her to stay behind, but she'd begged not to go. She wanted to see him over the summer. They told her she could make her own decisions. She promised she'd only take day trips to Chicago. Never stay the night.

Lachlan met her at the train station.

"Want to go out for supper? I just got paid." He pulled her into the crook of his clove-scented arm.

She didn't go home for the rest of the summer. Her parents called, emailed, showed up on the doorstep of Lachlan's horrible apartment building, her mother crying outside the smashed glass doors, refusing to come in. She begged her daughter to come home. But Madeline wanted to smoke and drink and be with Lachlan. She lost track of the days. Didn't go back to school in the fall. After six months of living with Lachlan, she no longer saw the mold. She no longer noticed the marks on his roommates' arms and, when she did, she dismissed them.

A year passed. Lachlan worked all day while she slept, too stoned and lazy to work. One morning she woke up and looked around. The bedroom was filthy, there were T-shirts and socks and underwear strewn across the floor. Empty cans of beer on the bed. She knew she'd wanted to finish high school. She'd wanted to go to college. But it was autumn, she'd missed the start of the school year again. She resolved to find work, get up early, call the school. That night, sick of not getting any pleasure from what they were smoking, Lachlan suggested something new.

"Give me your arm," Lachlan said.

"Just this once, okay?"

"Sure baby."

That first hit of heroin, a sensation never to be repeated again, was worth stealing, lying, even dying for. She would do things she'd bring herself to never admit to, questing for that same sensation. She was powerless over the hunger it created. It was like eating fine chocolate that scorched her taste buds so nothing ever tasted as good again.

Before long, Lachlan was out of work. He'd missed so many shifts, his father couldn't keep him on the construction site any longer. Out of the grab-bag of options they found themselves holding, taking things from other people's homes seemed like the one with the least amount of risk. She'd watched the girls on the streets of Englewood, hustling for hours only to come home bruised. She didn't want that. The first time she and Lachlan broke into a house, she was so nervous she threw up on the welcome mat. But before too long, breaking into homes had become commonplace. She knew the layout of those houses, felt her way around them in the dark with her eyes closed. She knew when to step over the ceramic dog bowl that lay beside the stainless-steel fridge, knew how far from the cupboards the island was located; where the laptop, cellphones and wallets were likely to be. And, most importantly, she had a good idea where people just like her parents would hide cash — in the freezer, under the utensil divider in the kitchen, or, of all places, in the underwear drawer.

Her biggest mistake the night she was arrested was going for the cash in the bedroom. Lachlan had warned her that she'd be backing herself into a corner if she wandered too far from a doorway. She thought she saw the whole family pull away in their SUV. When the homeowner flicked on the bedside lamp she'd stood motionless with her hand in his wife's underwear drawer.

THE LUNCH BELL WOKE Ashton up. He'd slept for forty-five minutes, good for a five-month-old. He was hungry. She placed his little plum-shaped face on her breast. His bone-marrow-coloured hair was damp and curly. His legs were ringed with scarlet from the elastics on the bottom of the onesie.

She was to hear from the governor's office within the hour. The State of the State Address would be broadcast and his budget announced. The other mothers were going to congregate in the playroom, turn the wooden rocking chairs to the screen, sit the children on the play mat, and watch anxiously.

The governor wanted to take their children away from them. What he doesn't know, or doesn't want to believe, is that most of them won't use again. Most of the women don't want to be separated from their children. There are a few who are incapable of staying clean, but most of them want a normal life more than anything.

The governor says they are bad people. He says they can't teach their children to be good citizens because they aren't capable of it themselves. He wants them to surrender their children to the state.

She can't send Ashton to Lachlan. He took a bullet in the head while trying to rob a corner store. She was in prison when she heard the news, his beautiful face on the evening news. She cried for weeks. She was in her seventh month. When she gave birth, she wrote *father unknown* on the record.

"WE'RE GOING TO GET you out of there," Madeline's father said after her sentencing.

She wanted to curl up in her mother's lap and go home now. But she couldn't respond to her father's assured statement. She couldn't look at her parents. The guards brought her to her cell and called her privileged. "Stupid princess," one said. "My kids have to work two jobs this summer to go to college and she stuffed the cost of it up her veins."

When she became aware of her pregnancy, she no longer wanted drugs — unequivocally and with no fuss. She tuned out the cravings and withdrawal like they were unnecessary words in a boring conversation. She coasted on a sense of grace. A whole new person was emerging, someone with a purpose outside of herself, someone imbued with a deep sense of peace and strength. Her own discomfort meant nothing. All that mattered was her baby. There was no way she was going to terminate her pregnancy or give up her child when she delivered it. She spent those months going to group therapy by day and reading books about taking care of a newborn at night. She wrote a letter to the governor. He didn't respond. She wrote a letter to Lachlan's parents. They didn't respond. She wrote a letter to her parents. They wrote back.

On their first visit Ashton was two days old. They surprised her with baby clothes and toys wrapped in tissue paper and placed in bags with blue ribbons. She'd gone through labour and delivery under police supervision at St. Mary's Hospital. She was all by herself, no husband or mother, under the care of grouchy nurses who treated her body like a cumbersome duffel bag. She'd cried the whole time; she was lonely and wanted her mother to be there, but was afraid of her disapproval. Would she be ashamed?

"He's just wonderful," her father said and nestled him gently in the crook of his arm. His hands trembled.

Her mother hung her head and wept quietly.

"I've built a playground in the backyard," her father said.

Her mother held Ashton against her chest tightly. "If they decide to close this program he can come home with us. We'll keep him until the end of your sentence." She stroked the top of Ashton's head.

"I'm sorry, Mom. I'm so sorry."

The group counsellor told the mothers to keep the focus on themselves. "Don't blame others for your choices," she'd said. She didn't blame them.

Being sentenced taught Madeline how to live again. Taught her how to be a good citizen. Giving Ashton stability was what she wanted now. She wanted to be with him, to hold him, to let him know that she loved him, not just when it was convenient, but all the time. Because when all is said and done, his life was here with her. In a home bordered by a barbed wire fence, but a home just the same. It was a normal baby's life; he ate and slept, and when he was awake he only had eyes for her.

The facilities were clean and bright. The walls of the children's room were plastered with coloured paper tulips in the spring and white paper snowflakes in the winter. The common room was filled with toys. She couldn't give him up. His home was with her.

WHEN THE GOVERNOR'S FACE appeared on the television, she hung her head, ashamed. She thought of the man's face in the last home she'd broken into. She ran out of his house and down the street and boarded a city bus. She had the notion of hiding on the beach for a few days. While she was there, she was going to figure everything out. Only Lachlan had come and she gave him what she'd taken from the house. He went away with the goods and came back with drugs. They'd shot up and before she knew it, she was asleep at the shoreline.

She watched the governor give his customary we-are-the-greatest-state-in-the-greatest-nation rally call, followed by a speech involving unemployment statistics, job creation plans, and budget figures. And, within a long list of items his government affirmed their continued support and investment in, she heard him list the Moms and Babies program.

Ashton could stay with her until her sentence was served.

She watched her baby fall asleep in her lap, kissed his nose, and wriggled her finger into the palm of his clenched fist. She rocked back and forth, her toes curling on the floor. Ashton yawned. Not a care in the world, oblivious to the importance of this moment.

In a year-and-a-half, when she is released, she will go home. She will live with her mother and father. They will take Ashton swimming in the summer; watch the people and boats and clouds. They will eat hot dogs with onions and ketchup. Share plates of fries. Drink sodas. The sand will stick to their toes and they'll track it indoors.

# *The Fresh Coast*

AN INSISTENT BUZZ WOKE North 'Spitz' Cumming. He rolled over. A crumpled Detroit Red Wings cap and a handful of chicken wing bones fell to the floor. He reached under his legs to free his cell. For the first time in months, he felt a surge of hope when he saw that Anahita was calling. He still loved her, but she'd let him go, threw him back like an unwanted fish.

She was crying.

"I can't cross the border," she said.

"Why not?"

"Iranians can't enter the US from Canada," said Anahita.

Did he hear her right? She couldn't come back to Michigan? In between sobs he heard her say that the president wasn't permitting entry by citizens from Islamic middle-eastern and North African countries.

North swallowed the knot, caused by guilt, forming in his throat. He had voted for him. Well of course he had, jobs were promised. His type of work in the cherry industry. How was he supposed to know that this would happen?

"I don't know when I'll be able to come back," said Anahita.

He said he'd come and get her this morning. No way would he fly. Yes, he knew the storm was coming. He pulled back the grey curtain in his dingy trailer and the limbs of the tamarack outside his window, sodden with clumps of slushy snow, were buckling. The lake-effect storm Traverse City had been expecting — broadcasters unrelenting with warnings that water and electricity could cease functioning, cars could become trapped underneath feet of snow, roads and banks and grocery stores would close — had started.

He'd be out of the worst of it within a few hours, he told her.

He took a quick shower and made coffee. Yesterday he didn't know if he would ever see or hear from Anahita again. But she'd called. He had a chance to win her back, a chance to show her how much he loved her.

He threw on a John Deere T-shirt and a pair of jeans, rooted through a pile of clothes for a pair of boots and a ski jacket. A quick phone call to work to let them know he wouldn't be coming in. Yep. The flu. He'd be out a few days at least.

His pickup truck barrelled through the snow on the uncleared roads and within minutes he was on the highway, but there his truck inched along, the storm slowing all manner of vehicles, even those he thought the weather wouldn't matter to. The heavy snow fell so quickly that his windshield wipers struggled under the load. He could barely see.

THE FIRST TIME HE saw Anahita, he was loading a cherry tank on a forklift. She was leading a group of college students through the orchard, there to study fungus, a by-product of the spring heat wave and subsequent frost which had wiped out ninety percent of that year's cherry crop.

They stopped to watch North, one of only two men in the orchard. He got out of the forklift to board and drive the cherry shaker, in tandem with the cherry receiver, alongside the rows of trees. The students trailed behind, watching the clamp encircle the tree, shake the fruit free, and rain it on the receiver's conveyor belt to be dumped in the tank. When the tank filled up, North got off and walked back to the forklift, removed the full tank and drove it to the trucks taking the cherries to the fruit factory to be washed, pitted, frozen and packed.

Usually quick, the processes were slow this harvest due to recent lay-offs. Because so many men lost their jobs and the owners, losing their minds, prayed to receive low-interest loans from the federal government, North bore the brunt of it. Doing the work of five harvesters, and helping out at the processing factory at night, deprived him of sleep. Insect repellant and a fetid slick of sweat fermenting underneath the dust on his skin, North nearly bumped into Anahita as she stood under a tree, a branch in her long thin hands, sculpted nails blister red, cupping a clump of cherries. When he met her eyes, ringed in black kohl, he inhaled sharply.

He said nothing. Not in possession of strong nerves, he avoided her warm brown eyes and bent to gather branches, clearing the way for her and the procession that followed. He didn't think she noticed him as he drove the forklift through the orchard.

He was driving men away from Anahita the first time she gave him any mind. A few weeks after that, Friday night at the Sail Inn, he and the boys were playing pool. Half-cut from an earlier visit to The Party Store, Scurvy McQuaid — a Yooper with a lazy eye — hustled half the men in the room and emptied their wallets quickly. North — smaller than anyone, but with fast fists and biceps that bulged when he lifted his beer — had been drinking since five and turned his head when she walked into the bar with the same crowd of fair-haired, plump, college girls. They sat a few tables away, giggling at the playlist on the karaoke machine, programming the evening away with pop songs. Scurvy smiled at one with red lipstick and moved in.

Anahita scowled when Scurvy sat at the table. She wasn't drinking the beer he'd sent over. The other girls accepted his round of drinks. After he gestured to the waitress, she put a smoked ham sandwich in front of Anahita. Anahita promptly took a scarf out of her bag and wrapped it around her head.

"It's just a sandwich. I'm being friendly here."

Anahita ignored him.

"Islamic bitch," Scurvy muttered loud enough for the table of girls to gasp as one. North stood up, fist in Scurvy's face before he could crack another one. The boys were on him, held him back from Scurvy who cupped his bleeding nose in disbelief. The girls scattered faster than cherries shaking loose from a tree.

North wrested himself free and followed Anahita.

Outside, he tried to open her car door but she pushed him away.

"I don't need your help," said Anahita.

"Okay," said North. He told her he'd seen her at the cherry orchard.

"Beautiful crop," said Anahita.

"They're my babies," said North and blurted out an invite. "Could I show you around? Take you out for a local treat — a hamburger? They're made with beef and cherries." Yes, he knew how to get to the University. Yes, he would meet her there.

NORTH HURRIED HOME AFTER school to meet his father. His father pulled up, red-eyed, stinking of whiskey after finishing his shift at the cannery. The trailer park was filled with snow, but North wore hi-top sneakers, ripped jeans, and a leather jacket.

His father made him put on a snowsuit. "Long Lake is colder than town," he said. "And we'll be out for a while. I want to catch as many as I can."

"Hungry?" his father asked when he got inside the truck and handed him a McDonald's bag. "Drink?" North waved away the bourbon and put his feet up on the ice fishing sled his father had thrown in the front.

"Get your feet off," he said and North crammed his feet in beside it.

They drove in silence. The forced air in the cabin smelled fusty, the one good windshield wiper pushed the trickle of wet flakes out of his father's line of vision. North's father gulped bourbon while humming a Whitesnake song. After driving for twenty minutes, pine branches scraping the side of the truck, the vehicle bouncing on the rough road, they saw that their usual fishing spot was, thankfully, deserted. They climbed out of the truck and piled supplies on the sled.

Once the ice was drilled, North, as clumsy as a three-legged dog, dropped his father's line in the water.

"Christ," his father said and took a swing, clubbing North on the side of the head. North fell on the ice and watched droplets of blood spill out of his nose. A few kicks in the stomach and North curled like a salted leech.

Prone on the ice, he mistook the slamming of his father's truck door as a newly arrived vehicle. He pushed himself to sitting and wiped his nose. He rose to his feet, his father saluting him with his middle finger, sneering at North in the rearview mirror.

Limping home, an hour's walk alone in the falling snow, he found the door to the trailer open. His mother, an ice-pack over a swollen eye, picked up her suitcase, "Don't worry kid," she said. "There's a chicken pot pie in the oven." She walked out the door. Her jewelry box was open on the table, most of the contents gone. The one item remaining in its red faux-velvet box was the cheap cameo his father had bought for his mother, the most romantic thing a Union man born-and-raised in the Mitten could have done.

AFTER THREE HOURS OF driving, nose to end with transports and cars flicking up wet snow, North needed to get off the road and grab something to eat. He passed a sign announcing the exit for a gas station. There were a few hotels clustered around the highway exit, which made him long for more sleep. He yearned for Anahita's warm body curled beside him in bed. He thought of her beautiful face, profile like the image on his mother's cameo. North had given her his mother's cameo and she'd laughed and called it old-fashioned.

North pulled into the parking at the first restaurant. Two men in dark ski-jackets were hunched at a table, warming their hands on cups of coffee. The grey-haired waitress asked North what he wanted. She poured him coffee and asked him to speak up if he was going to order breakfast. He didn't like speaking in public. He wrapped his hands around the hot mug and listened as the man on the stool beside him, white beard yellowed from smoke residue, chatted with the waitress. North longed to join in the easy banter between the two. They must have known each other well, as the man teased the waitress, bragging about trips on his snowmobile over icy lakes that were known to contain soft parts. She was sassy with him, spurring him on to bigger and bolder tales. To be a man like that, fearless around women, confident, he was certain they had it easier. North's cellphone dinged. A text from his father asking if he would buy him some groceries before the storm shut everything down. North put his hand over his mouth. He'd forgotten about his father. He sent a message to the volunteer at the Lighthouse Church of God, who delivered food to the seniors in the King's Court Trailer Park, asking her to make sure his father had water and food. He pressed send and his phone went dead. Had the message gone through? No way to check now.

North paid his bill and smiled at the waitress who looked back at him without expression.

Back in the truck, he realized he'd forgotten his charger. He'd buy one the next time he stopped. Once on the road again, he cursed the length of time that remained. He began to feel anxious. In spite of their last fight, he couldn't wait to see Anahita and bring her home.

"HOME?"

North had asked Anahita where home was.

"Toronto. My parents are there," responded Anahita. Distracted by a piece of cherry in her ice cream cone, she didn't tell him where she and her parents had left to get to Toronto. He was pretty sure Canadians didn't speak with her accent. Anahita rolled the cherry on her tongue, assessing its flavour. He'd picked her up at six o'clock, showered twice before getting himself out the door, and sped all the way to the University. But he couldn't get out of the car to approach her office until he took a shot of the bourbon he kept in the glove compartment.

She told him that she'd grown up on a small cherry orchard in Iran. Her father's operation was so small he picked the cherries by hand. Her fondest memories of childhood included the smell on warm summer nights of hookah, her mother's talc, figs and dates, and cherry bars baking. They lived in Iran until a government inspector who smuggled produce cut her father out of the market. They immigrated to Canada in the early nineties and settled in Toronto, living in an apartment building that had black mold and bed bugs. It was the neighbourhood where a man chopped his daughter into pieces and threw her remains in the lake. Her father drove a taxi twelve hours at a time, sometimes during the day and sometimes at night, suffering the much-repeated well-meaning question "Where are you from" and all its implications — "You don't belong here" — and worse, the insults spat at him, the frequent thefts. Her mother rolled falafel balls all day at Ali Baba's. Anahita had earned scholarships to go to university and had eventually completed her doctorate at the University of Guelph. Shortly after, she accepted the offer of an associate professorship at Michigan State's Horticultural Research Center. And, yes, she liked it here. Yes, she liked her job.

"Why do they call you 'Spitz'?"

He picked a cherry from his cone and looked at it carefully before eating. He inspected another too bruised to eat, and put it on a napkin. He told her he was a local hero, the International Cherry Spitting Champion; he could spit a pit over ninety feet.

"How is that possible?" asked Anahita.

He winked and told her he had great oral skills.

After dinner they went to an art exhibit by the lake. It featured local artists' paintings, acrylics depicting Lake Michigan's sand dunes, various marinas, waterfowl, and wildlife. She admired a handbag made from recycled fruit sacks and he purchased it for her. She slung it over her shoulder proudly.

"Would you like to come over for coffee?"

Inside his trailer, Anahita stepped over mounds of his things: broken fishing rods, rusted augers, dented campfire crockery,

Coleman gas lanterns, frayed fishing nets, a pair of rain pants — the strap held together with black tape — and a blunted ice chisel.

"All of it, junk," said North.

"My mother keeps everything. Even the most useless items," said Anahita.

As she crouched to inspect his boots, she told him about a Persian folk tale her mother loved, "The Faith of a Starving Man." A Dervish, lost in the desert, finds useless items, none of which feed his hunger. No matter this, he gives thanks to God for providing him with an empty fruit sack, a hunting bow with no string, the branches from a barren fruit tree, a dented pot, and an old hook. Eventually, he reaches a wide river, which he can't cross on his own. Here, he falls to his knees and thanks God for all that he has. In a moment of clarity, he ties the hook and the broken string to the hunting bow to use as a fishing rod, catches a fish, and cooks it in the old pot over a fire made from the dried tree branches.

"Everything has a purpose, even if we can't see it at the time," said Anahita.

"My mother said stuff like that too, said she'd fallen in love with my father because he was unwanted and she felt compassion for him. But I think some things are just trash," said North.

"Then why don't you throw this out?"

"I can't. My father gave me that ice fishing gear."

Anahita put her feet up on the ice fishing sled his father had made thirty years ago.

"Don't put your feet on that."

"Why not? It's just junk."

"My father made it out of his old shed."

"My point exactly," said Anahita.

"WHAT IS YOUR POINT?" asked one of Anahita's professor friends.

"The shorelines of large bodies of water are immeasurable because of the coastline paradox," said a hydrology professor. "Coastlines, like borders, change shape due to erosion."

"Proof of irreducibility," a female professor said.

"Subjectivity," said another.

North told them that Lake Michigan was part of the world's largest group of freshwater lakes and that's why it was called the Fresh Coast. "Eureka!" one woman shouted. "Oh, that's why," another said. The men in the conversation acted as if they had known all along, but were content to let North, the least educated of the group, reveal the information.

The bright sun, life jacket red, moved along the lengthy expanse of the shores of Lake Michigan and sunk, deflated, into the seam of a precise horizon line. North would have told them that the section of the lake closest to the horizon is called the *offing* if conversation hadn't taken a turn.

At the mention of borders, a pudgy male professor with a globular mole under his earlobe brought the conversation around to contemporary politics. A topic North had grown accustomed to ignoring. Of course, he hadn't voted for her, but over time he'd learned to keep his mouth shut. He was being especially careful this weekend, because they were staying in a luxurious beach house in Grand Haven, which had been built for the host's grandfather, one of Kennedy's public policy advisors.

"What else can we do but eat sheet cake?" A professor asked in her best Tina Fey voice; she laughed and handed out forks.

In the dim light of the evening, the lake, ten feet from the patio, dark as a blackberry, lapped against the dock and underneath churned grains of sand away from the shoreline, gently and slowly eroding it. The conversation turned again, this time to a topic with which North was most uncomfortable; how did he, a man with no education, who juggled two jobs in the cherry industry, capture the attentions of the beautiful, the exotic, the intelligent Anahita? Anahita laughed and said he had great oral skills.

NORTH'S MOUTH WAS DRY. It was dark and the roads were icy. He was approaching Port Huron and the border, after an eight-hour drive that should have been four. He pulled off the highway and rented a room in a cheap motel. He needed to find a Wal-Mart to buy a charger.

"Use your email for a second?" he asked the older woman at the front desk.

She shook her head, wagged her finger at him and shooed him out of the lobby. He drove to the closest Wal-Mart to find it closed due to flooding. Hungry and tired, he gave up and went for dinner at a steakhouse, drank himself into a stupor, stumbled back to the motel, and fell into bed after midnight, without word to anyone.

He woke quickly the next morning, skipped having a shower, coffee and breakfast. He dressed, checked out, got in the car and drove. In the distance, he could see the bridge and the border crossing. The snowdrifts on the grey rock of the shoreline looked like hundreds of cows lying end-to-end. Would Anahita be angry that he hadn't called? Would this cause another fight? After their last one she looked at him in disgust; as if he hadn't quite grown up yet, as if he was still toting a mickey of whiskey in his duffel bag, as if he still wore a baseball cap backwards.

Anahita was working late at the University the last time he saw her, preparing lecture notes for the following day. North watched her through the window in her office from the street.

He waited until all her colleagues had left. He walked in, face red with blood. Anahita was trimming the ends of a bouquet of red roses he'd sent, thorns like mosquito noses. Even though they nipped at her tiny fingers, she was smiling contentedly — little bites no need for concern — that is until she saw North. Her brow furrowed.

North, she whispered, dropped the roses and sat him at her desk. She wiped his wounds, murmured words of comfort. North sat on the chair and burrowed his head in her chest, hands tugging at her shoulder blades. She rubbed his hair for a moment then lifted his face.

"What have you done?"

"They called you a —"

"Beating them won't make them stop."

"I should let them insult you?"

North said he'd do anything for her, no matter what. Told her he loved her more than anything. He always would. Anahita turned her face away.

"I can't go on like this," she said.

Three weeks later on a Sunday afternoon, not a word from Anahita since the night at the University, he sat on the orange vinyl seat of his sled drilling the ice with his auger. He assembled his fishing line and dropped it in the water. Alone on the frozen stream next to the interstate. Cars trundled by, the caustic smell of exhaust hovered.

A bottle of Woodward Bourbon Whiskey the only thing he'd put his lips on since she'd left. He'd called and begged. Come back woman, I'll settle myself. I don't understand all this machismo, she'd said. She didn't know what the old boys were capable of, thought she didn't need him to protect her. Scurvy'd do more than make fun of her diet if he had his way. Just picturing him hurting her compelled North to drive over to Scurvy's yesterday with his rifle. He shot out the tires from under his truck. Anahita would never know he'd done that. But she sure wouldn't be bothered by Scurvy when he found out she was single.

The line on his rod wavered, tightened, then slackened. That one got away, thought North. Grief gnawed at him. He had tried inviting women over, the ones that sold their services online, and what they did on their knees, although pleasurable, couldn't assuage his emptiness. He hadn't expected to love her so much. A few months ago, when she told him she loved him, he felt something sharp and piercing, an attachment he'd never experienced before. He didn't want to compare Anahita with his mother, or the love he felt to the memory of the love he'd felt for her. Felt. He no longer knew, loved, or cared about his mother. She was gone. And that was all he would give over to comparison.

He'd never tell his father he'd fallen in love with an Iranian woman.

A car drove by on the interstate and honked. One of the boys from the Sail Inn. North raised a gloved hand and saluted. He'd meet the boys there later, smooth things over with a compliant Scurvy, drink, chase an easy lay, bring her home, ask her to make breakfast, because God knows, he should eat something.

Why worry? Why pine for someone gone? Nothing to be gained. If she's gone and she doesn't look back, forget about her. North took another swig of whiskey and got up from the chair on the sled, reeled in the line and crossed the stream, sled dragging behind him.

THE ICE FISHING SLED banged against North's heels as he pulled it down the incline, on the icy banks of the St. Clair River. He'd taken the contents from his truck — auger, pot, rod — and threw them in to make it look like he was ice fishing. Anahita waited for him in the truck, worried and scared and cold.

He'd arrived in Toronto yesterday, four hours later than expected. She cried when she saw him.

"The roads are so icy," she'd said and told him she couldn't stop imagining the worst, scenes of him careening off the road and crashing into roadside trees, freezing to death, buried beneath pine boughs.

"The drive was fine," he'd said and held her tightly.

But it hadn't been. He'd rolled along slowly, southern Ontario under siege from its own storm, snow butting his windshield. Passing signs read *Fatigue kills! Take a break!* and *It's not summer!* He'd laughed; in his hometown roadside warnings were futile. His friends wouldn't take heed in their pickup trucks, or snowmobiles. They'd knock them down and use them for firewood. North didn't dare take his eyes off the road until he parked outside of Anahita's parents' co-op.

"You weren't kidding about the potholes," North said.

"Only two seasons in Toronto: winter and construction," her father said and held out his hand.

Anahita's mother served him endless plates of food.

"America must be the greatest nation on earth," said her father.

"Are the maternity hospitals affordable?" her mother asked.

North's heart leapt. The thought of it.

ANAHITA'S MOTHER PREPARED PAANI kam chai tea and poured it in paper cups to take as they walked through the neighbourhood in the white stillness after the storm. They climbed the bridge over the new West End Rail Path in the Junction Triangle. Directly below them, a new townhouse development rose out of the pit of a former paint factory. They were surrounded by buildings that once held postwar manufacturers; brown brick structures embossed with white paint advertising aluminum, tarp, and textiles.

"Why is there a giant cock in the sky?" North asked and pointed to the CN Tower in the distance.

Anahita scowled and asked him to refrain from vulgarities.

A westerly wind tugged on Anahita's hair and alternately scattered the strands and flattened them against her cheeks.

"I want to marry you," North said.

Anahita's eyes watered from the searing wind.

"Did I hear you right?" she said.

He nodded.

"I'll marry you if you get me home."

Early the next morning, North wasted no time. They got in his truck and headed back to the U S of A. On the drive to the border crossing over the St. Clair River, they stopped for coffee at the Tim Hortons in Brantford. North was beside himself to be in Gretzky's hometown. He recited hockey stats until they turned on Highway 402. An hour later they could see the Blue Water Bridge emerging in the distance, its lights still on. Anahita pointed out the bowstring arch over the bridge.

"Well, you've got your fruit sack," North said and pointed to the handbag in her lap, the one he bought for her at the art exhibit. "There's your bow string bridge, and I've got an old pot and ice fishing hooks in the back of the truck and I'm taking you to a river so wide you can't possibly cross it on your own," North said.

"Not a bad interpretation for an American. Faith in you and I will not starve," Anahita said and laughed.

"I'm not completely useless," North said. "But you will get cold and wet."

"Why?"

They veered off the main road and drove through a few small townships until they were just outside of Sombra. They passed the ferry terminal.

"Am I taking this boat?" Anahita asked.

"No, you're going to cross on a smaller one," North said. He drove on by and pulled to a stop in front of an A-frame cottage on the shoreline. A black-haired man, taller than his own doorframe stepped out of the house and waved.

"My ice fishing buddy is going to take you across the river. I'm going to meet you on the other side," said North.

"You're smuggling me across?"

"Yep."

"We'll get caught," she said and burst into tears.

He told her his friend was a border guard. "He'll get you across the river in less than twenty minutes. I'll sit here and keep watch, but we better hurry, he told me a freighter is due in thirty minutes."

"We'll get caught."

The man approached, ushered them inside, handed Anahita a navy jacket like his and a large hat, told her to tuck up her hair. North returned to where he'd left the ice sled on the banks of the St. Clair, dropped his line in the semi-frozen water and watched them step into the motorized dinghy. They set out slowly, dodging chunks of moving ice.

Nervous, North lost his line in the powerful current. He experienced initial panic, habitual since childhood, whenever he did something wrong, especially when ice fishing, but quickly regained his composure. He isn't here, he thought. It doesn't matter if I drop my line, lose all my tackle, or the whole goddamn ice sled. He's not here, he can't hit me. I'm in charge now.

Was she trembling? Was it just the wind ruffling her jacket? The dinghy was moving quickly, it seemed to bounce over the current. His friend had said, "I do this all the time, I offer fish to the coast guards and they turn a blind eye." But still, that bounce. The height on it. The dinghy would roll over if the wind caught it just right. A blast caught North's breath. He saw Anahita reach up to clutch her hat, her body wobbling as she let go of the boat. He couldn't hear the electric razor-like motor anymore, only the yowl of the wind whittling the large slabs of snow drift anchored to the frozen shore.

Eventually, he saw that the dinghy had made it all the way across. She'd crossed the river. He did it. He'd brought her back. Home. To North. Where she belonged. North kicked his ice sled into the river. The current caught it quickly and dragged it only a few feet before it sank.

He was going to marry her, there was no way he'd let her slip through his fingers. He'd muzzle his fists if that's what she wanted, cut ties with all his drinking buddies. His love was as vast as a shoreline, but it would never erode or change shape. It was immeasurable, deep and wide like the water in the lake.

# *Ebb*

SOME SAY THAT MY sisters and I are plus-sized, but I prefer the term *filled-out*. As in *she fills out her jeans* or *her hips are filled out*. We all look similar, share the same dark hair and wide-set brown eyes. I would say we are all strong, despite our girth, have large, flat hands — an oddity people have been marvelling about our whole lives — and our collar bones are as thick as pipes. We have stout necks, full of veins that pulse when one of us says something. And we are all talkers. And Dad needed to talk to us.

The three of us, Olivia, Vanessa, and me, Aurora, are spending the evening at our father's house, in our hometown of Killarney. Our father, Ebb — a shortened version of his full name, Ebenezer, a name he always hated — is hosting his own retirement party. He stands at the grill, flipping pork chops, "These expensive ones from that natural farmer. He lets the sows live a normal life, they don't suffer."

Olivia hands Vanessa a bowl of bean salad.

"How many wieners are there?" I ask worriedly and rise to count the chops on the grill.

"This spread must have cost you a lot, let me help," Vanessa says and reaches for her purse.

"No. Keep your money. I've got it," Olivia says cheerfully.

"I want to tell you something before the guests arrive," Dad says.

"Yes?" I ask, as my sisters fuss over where to place the bread on the picnic table. Dad sprays the flames of a grease fire and closes the lid on the barbecue. He sits on the lip of the picnic table, one eye on us, the other on the smoke rolling out from under the lid.

"There's something I've been thinking about every day since I retired."

I NEVER USED TO count the steps home, but after that day I did, wondering if I could have timed it better, got home earlier, or arrived a few minutes later. Maybe I wouldn't have seen what I saw. It took three hundred and fifty-nine steps from school to our house, a bungalow at the dead end of Channel Street. The white paint had faded, was flushed with speckles of mold, as if someone had thrown a handful of dirt at the walls. My mother was inside, on the couch, round as a mushroom. My father was at work in Killarney National Park, more at home in the bog, amongst the trees, preferring to take care of the saplings, recording the habits of the lichens and mosses on the round smooth boulders that border Obatanga River, than staying home with his ill wife.

Step seventy-three: a few boys and girls from my class on their way home, standing on the side of the road.

"Want to come and play soccer?" a boy asked.

"She can't. Her mom needs a diaper change," another said.

I hung my head. Said nothing. As was instructed.

Step eighty-nine: pumpkin-orange leaves fell from the trees and twirled in concentric spirals. I brushed them from my shoulders. Mom told me that she hated trees, hated the great outdoors, and even hated the sluggish river that snaked in the channel.

Mom had been diagnosed with multiple sclerosis and then sleep apnea. They gave her a machine that looked like a World War II gas mask, the hose clamped to her head with a rubber snout sending purified air to her nose. She slept peacefully. No more grunting or rearing her head, half-awake in the night, gasping for breath. But that was only one problem solved. Some days, she couldn't walk; the fatigue was immobilizing.

Dad had read an article that said Canada, particularly Northern Ontario, had high rates of MS. Mom blamed the lack of sunlight; a neighbour blamed mosquitoes; a nurse at the clinic blamed carbon emissions. Another neighbour, one who suffered from asthma, blamed the smoke from leaves people burned in their backyards in the fall.

Step three-hundred-one: at the corner of our street. I waved to the owner of Herbert's Fisheries — a fish-and-chips restaurant — who was stooped over a pile of leaves, igniting them, protecting the tiny flame from the extinguishing breeze. He winked. Apple-red flames came to life and licked and curled leaves. Grey smoke coiled above, thin and swift. I inhaled and wrinkled my nose.

My sisters were at a basketball tournament. We'd left Mom this morning, alone, asleep on the sofa, a wheelchair catalogue at her feet. When I got home, the back door was ajar. I poked my head around the corner to see inside the living room. She was half-hidden amongst the afternoon shadows. She didn't like the lights on in the house. The living room had what looked like an oxygen deprived blue-grey pallor.

Dad was giving her pills one at a time. She swallowed each of them, almost choking once. I don't know how many she took. To this day when the scene arrives, unbidden in my memory, I count them over and over, but I can't arrive at a total. He lay down with her and held her. Her breath, in gasps and grunts, sounded so much like her breathing before the sleep apnea diagnosis that at the time I hadn't quite put two and two together until he got up and called the ambulance.

DAD TELLS US WHAT he wants to do now that he's retired, and there's a story behind it, too, which makes it all the more exciting for him.

"A man from Michigan came in to Tim's the other day and asked where he could get a grilled hot dog. I told him to go to the mall; he was shocked. 'You can only get hot dogs at the mall?' he says. 'Not in the park or in the street?' he says, and then it hit me. This town needs a hot dog stand. So I decided that I am going to open Killarney's very first hot dog stand."

"A hot dog stand?" Olivia says and her face betrays her thoughts. She thinks she's better than all of us and I'm sure this venture embarrasses her. She's all fur coat and no knickers — something Mom's family back in Scotland said — because she just bought a brand-new four-bedroom home. Custom-made by Ivan's Building Company. Last week, she told me she is falling in love with Ivan.

Ivan had built her a dream home on a rugged plot of land. On a math teacher's salary. I don't know how she afforded it, but having something other people will envy is Olivia's ambition. She likes to splash cash around. She's good at playing posh.

She told me Ivan was a good three inches shorter than her five foot eight, but she could overlook that due to other assets like his strong arms and muscular chest. While he was building the house, he waited for her at the end of each day. She drove to the lot straight from school and nitpicked at the men while they worked. She was tired at the end of the day and knew that she looked it. "Why he was attracted to me in this state I'll never know," she said to me on the phone. Once inside the house, she demanded to see the floor plans, measured the rooms to see if they were the correct dimensions, and then argued viciously with Ivan about costs. She told me that Ivan liked to haggle and she knew he loved it when she named her price. She felt his admiration for her from day one.

When her house was nearly done, Ivan poured my sister a glass of wine and sat with her beside the freshly stained stairwell and stroked her toes. "I'm in love with you," he'd said. "You should give me a try." She'd give him a go only if he kept a successful business, she didn't want to associate with any slacker, she said. And he laughed and raised his toe to her lips.

"It'll be easy to get you a small business loan, Dad. You'll need money for equipment and supplies," Vanessa says.

Of all of us I knew that she'd be the one who'd be excited about the news. A businesswoman to the core, kept the same job in the TD Bank downtown that she got as soon as she graduated from college. Blunt, practical, and offended by disorder, she told me, quite proudly, that she always balanced her till at the end of the day and never gave in to customer complaints, because in her mind the numbers were always right. Ruthlessly moral, she caught three interns trying to steal last summer and reported them without a second thought.

She told me when she rolled over and saw her husband, Jerry, this morning, the black hair on his chest curling from humidity, she was angrier than she'd ever been. He slipped out on her again last night. It would be easier, she said, if it were drink or cards, but no, the man's other love was the moon and stars. He'd kept a telescope on the roof and spent his nights up there taking notes, measuring and calculating distances, mumbling about the cosmos in his sleep when he came back to bed at five or six in the morning. She told me she lay awake night after night, longing for his body heat and the weight of his thigh on her belly. He used to sling one leg over her and hold her head in the crook of his arm when they were first married, and she felt like the centre of the universe. Now she felt like invisible matter.

"Don't have more than three hundred hot dogs in stock at a time, because when there are over three hundred people at the casino, no one wins. And have six-hundred-forty-six serviettes at all times. Anytime six-four-six comes up, it's lucky. I've seen so many people win after these numbers come up it's not even funny," I say.

My sisters and father turn to stare at me with narrowed brows.

They don't understand me at all. I am a dealer at the casino in Sudbury. I allow only four keys on my keychain at a time, park in the sixth spot every day, and spend exactly one-hundred-six dollars at the grocery store each week, tallying the costs and adding the taxes while soldiering up and down the aisles. Uneven gram listings on cans appall me. I put them back, even when they are an essential ingredient for a dinner my husband, Bill, an Ontario Provincial Police officer, planned to make.

What they don't realize, and wouldn't believe me if I told them, is that if I put five keys on my keychain or if I park in the number nine spot, the seniors lose. I know this for a fact. It always happens.

If you don't believe me, just ask Don McGuinty. He comes in regularly and wins six hundred or so each month. Last week, he asked if I would feed his dog, Labbatt, while he went on vacation. He gave me the key to his greenhouse — he has the sturdiest morning glories in town — and offered free hothouse tomatoes in exchange for house-minding.

I slipped his key on my keychain attached to the lanyard around my neck. My regular customers lost for three straight weeks — until Don asked for his key back. When I gave him back his key, my customers started to win again.

"I can help. The bank offered ...," Vanessa says.

"Don't do it Dad, it'll be too much work," Olivia says.

"Make sure you chop an even number of onions for the condiment trays," I say.

He rises to take the pork chops off the barbecue.

A FEW WEEKS LATER, on June fourth, at four o'clock — I'd convinced him that the date of his grand opening should contain the numbers six and four — Dad stands at the end of his new cart and ignites the barbecue. He set the cart up across the street from the house, next to Herbert's Fish & Chips. At this time of day, the river sparkles. Regina, a reporter from the community newspaper, takes a photo to commemorate the opening of the town's first hot dog stand.

It's plain to see she has a crush on Dad. It's all over her face. The way she looks at him, smiles as he stacks wieners on the grill, the way she trips over herself to assist him with the condiment display.

"Nice shot. We'll put this one on the front page."

"How nice of you," he says and brushes her away as if she were a fly.

Relief flashes over his wizened face as she takes a step back. I don't think my father is a fool, he knows she likes him, but he's uncomfortable with it, as if he has too many things on one plate, and her presence is a dish he doesn't want to try.

"Want a sausage?"

"Love one!" she says and takes a step toward him. Olivia walks over and hugs Dad. Then introduces us to Ivan, who's been standing beside her patiently. He seems likeable enough, if you don't mind drywall plaster on your palms after a handshake. And then Vanessa is beside us.

She sidled up so quietly and speaks so softly we barely hear her when she says, "Congrats on the new cart, it's fabulous. I have an announcement of my own, I've been meaning to tell you that the bank made me ..."

"Smile," Regina says and snaps another photo. "We'll put this in the paper too, Ebb's first customers."

My husband, Bill, arrives shortly after, carrying his motorcycle helmet under one arm. He eats two dogs. Ivan says he wished that the cart sold beer. I want to count the wieners.

"You should slice these four times per dog and have an even number on the grill at all times," I say. No one responds.

When we say goodbye and walk to our cars, Olivia whispers, "Can't Regina tell Dad's not interested? Think she's going to charm him?"

"The odds of that happening are not high," I say and snort.

"She's a shameless flirt," Vanessa says.

I drop by after an overnight shift a week later. Dad wears a foam hat in the shape of a hot dog in a bun.

"If Olivia saw you in that she'd be mortified," I say.

"It would turn her stomach, wouldn't it?"

The mayor's son, a medical student at McMaster home for the summer, jogs along the boardwalk. He stops beside us.

"Water? Veggie dog with hot peppers?" Dad asks.

He gives him a thumbs up and leans over, hands on his hips, to catch his breath. Dad's friend from the park drops by and orders a sausage. As they catch up, I count his till. It's an odd total: eighty-five dollars and thirty-nine cents. Threes, fives and nines are ominous in my opinion, but I keep quiet.

Regina arrives and Dad serves her lunch.

"Got a great shot of the lake this morning," she says.

"Is that right," Dad says. He laughs at her because she's the sort of photographer who gets up early and climbs a tree to take pictures of the sunrise.

I HEAD OVER AGAIN next Saturday afternoon. Dad's foam hot dog hat bobs in the breeze as he serves the mayor's son his usual.

"I'm running out of buns," Dad says when I get out of my car.

"I'll go."

"No, watch the cart. It's a slow day. I'll get coffee while I'm at it," Dad says and hands me his apron.

I stand behind the cart. The red and white striped canopy flaps overhead. The barbecue gleams. His little radio made of black plastic, connected block letters that spell out "radio" plays the CBC. An empty Tim Hortons coffee cup sits beside it.

I serve Mrs. McKnight, a toddler on one hip and an infant strapped to her chest. I am so preoccupied with serving — making sure she has enough napkins, a straw in her orange pop — that I don't see the grease fire start on the grill, wieners in its grip, fat snapping and meat curling, napkins on the edge of the grill tray igniting. I don't know what to do. I turn off the gas and stand away from the propane tanks. I open a bottle of water and throw it on the fire. The fire leaps, scorching the canopy overhead. It tears at the material, burning it off the pole; bits of it fall to the ground. I put my hands over my mouth as the rest of it collapses.

THAT EVENING, VANESSA, OLIVIA, and I share a pot of coffee in Dad's kitchen. I count the grains of sugar Olivia spilled.

"You really ought to see someone about that. I know a doctor who ..."

"There are more important things going on right now," Olivia says silencing Vanessa. She pours more coffee into her purple floral mug.

Dad enters the kitchen. The focus shifts, all eyes are on him. He will settle everything; he has a certain way of getting things done, delegating, organizing.

"Let's make supper. Olivia, get the eggs. Vanessa fry the bacon. Aurora," he looks at me crouched over the table, picking up each grain of sugar with the tip of my finger. "Darling? You really ought to see someone about that."

I write the number of grains I'd counted on a piece of paper, put down the pen and rise to get the cutlery. Olivia blows the rest of the sugar off the table. I wince, but continue to set the table.

"Can't believe I forgot the fire extinguisher," Dad says.

"I knew all along that something would happen," Olivia says.

"Why don't you sell the cart? If you invest the money from the sale you can ..."

I interrupt Vanessa and say, "The till had an uneven float. Of course something bad happens when you let odd numbers dominate."

Dad is half-listening, massaging his thigh. He'd been complaining about sharp pains in his thigh since he opened the cart. A wooden cane, thick as a birch tree, rests by the arm of his chair. Regina had made it for him, presented it to him last week, told us that she sanded it herself and glued a thick amethyst on the handle. An amethyst she'd picked up outside of Thunder Bay, while driving to Winnipeg last summer.

"Selling the cart would be the ...," Olivia says and puts a pillow behind his back.

"Try to do your exercises at 6:06 in the morning, it's a lucky time, it will help your legs get stronger," I say.

"I'm not selling. I'm going to fix the cart," Dad says.

Vanessa says, "I've got good news, the bank promoted me in the spring ..."

"Look who's coming," Olivia, who's looking out the kitchen window, says. She's not aware that she's interrupted Vanessa again.

We cluster around and can't help but laugh. Regina is coming down the street towards the house.

"It's six o'clock, that's a good time of day too," I say and whistle slowly. All three turn away from the window to look at me.

"Don't be mean," Dad says.

"I BAKED A PEACH pie," Regina says as Dad opens the door.

He looks at the pie, turns, and walks back to the kitchen. Regina steps into the house, closes the door, and follows him.

"I'll take that," Olivia says.

"How many peaches did you put in this pie?" I ask.

Olivia elbows me in the ribs and walks away. Vanessa puts the kettle on the stove and motions for Regina to sit. We keep our backs to Dad and Regina who sit across from one another at the kitchen table. Olivia widens her eyes. Vanessa shrugs her shoulders. I busy myself cutting even-numbered slices of pie. It's a beautiful one. The crescent-shaped peach slices are amber and the crust crumbles like a child's biscuit. I pull out five plates from the cupboard: porcelain white plates decorated with peach-faced lovebirds, spearmint-green chests with rosy feathers.

"Not those," Vanessa whispers.

"Dad gave those to mom," Olivia says.

I put them back in the cupboard. With a slice of pie and a cup of tea prepared for each of us, Dad takes a deep breath.

"You are a great support, Regina. But I just don't feel the way you want me to."

"It's alright. I understand," she says and looks at us, forks in mid-air, mouths open.

"Give up on me. You've waited around far too long. I'm not going to change my mind."

"Ebb —"

"I value your friendship. You can have free hot dogs as long as I'm in business, but I can't offer you more than that."

"Ebb, you've got crumbs on your chin," she says.

He wipes them off and puts down his fork.

"And another thing, I'm not selling my cart. It's what I'm going to do as long as I can stand. I'm glad you got a promotion at work Vanessa, but this is the work I want to do."

"You heard me," Vanessa says and smiles.

"You can't continue working at that cart …," Olivia says.

"I'm not ashamed of my post-retirement career choice."

Olivia looks away.

"And I'm not hiring help. I can do it myself."

I wave my hands in surrender.

The doorbell rings. Ivan, Jerry, and Bill, back from their golf game, I suspect. I get up to answer it. The men come in and sit down. Regina gets up quietly and sneaks out the door. I follow her and watch her figure retreat down the street.

Even though we treat Dad like Vanessa — we're all in the habit of not listening to him as well as we should — he is as proud as Olivia and obsessive in his pursuits like me, single-minded and focussed, we should know better than to underestimate him once he makes up his mind. Mom was the same way.

"I'm glad she's gone," Olivia says behind me.

"She put too many peaches in that pie," I say.

"She should sell those pies, she'd make a lot of money if she ...," Vanessa starts to say, but Dad calls us. The men want pie. And he isn't going to serve them himself.

# Muddying the Waters

UNATTENDED, THEIR LAWN HAD fallen into disarray. Once green and lush, the envy of the street, the grass behind the house now sprouted dandelions, clover, and stinging nettles. I hadn't asked, but my husband William — full of information about foliage and waterfowl, always nattering on about trivialities — told me that with rapid reproduction rates, nettles were the most troublesome of weeds and very hard to eliminate.

I was angry; the nettles were on the verge of flowering and I feared they might spread to our backyard. Although, earlier in the summer I would have spread more than just my arms to welcome our new neighbours — well, him really — to the street. I'm ashamed to admit this now, but if you want the truth, there it is.

I'd just woken up. William was at work. The day, mine to do whatever I wanted with, was warm and the breeze subtle. I might have sunk into another fugue state, deliberate on my part, consisting of long swims and slow pontoon rides which effectively whittled away the afternoon — because who would want to remember the events of the past month? But the sounds of the moving van next door, four men shouting and expressing surprise at the weight of hauling the rest of John and Pauline's furniture out the patio door, down the deck and into the van, were invasive.

I parted the curtain and looked through the kitchen window. I wished I hadn't. John's brother, at least the man I was looking at who I assumed was John's brother, looked astonishingly like him except I couldn't see his eyes from this distance. If he'd had eyes like John's I wouldn't have met them. I'd be too frightened and I'd have looked away. John's eyes were navy blue when angry — more often than not, mainly because of his wife Pauline — and turquoise blue when pleased. They'd have turned the deepest navy if I'd told him that I'd seen her with another man.

A SUNDAY AFTERNOON IN early June, I sat on the edge of the dock watching John in his backyard, legs dangling in the clammy water. I wondered if I should tell him. A green water snake slithered across my toe. I yelped and brushed my right foot over the toe, attempting to erase the awful residual sense. John looked up and waved. Just a snake, I yelled. John was unloading fishing and hunting gear from his truck. The muscles in his back, lithe ribbons of flesh, rippled as he moved. Shirtless and in tight jeans, black hair in a slick vintage-style pompadour, he was easily the best-looking man in these parts.

My husband, William, and I are nowhere near as attractive as our neighbours. William is as rotund as a black bear. He has an elfin face: pointed dimpled chin and wide set oval eyes. I am stocky with a narrow head and soft, dumpy shoulders. Everyone calls me Oops; I'm the youngest of six children, the only girl in a family of five brothers. I'm pretty sure that I was a mistake.

We've lived here since we graduated from Laurentian and took jobs at the bank. A year ago, William was promoted head of Corporate Accounts and given a big pay raise. I immediately quit work. We were living the good life: a split-level bungalow on the banks of the Wanapitei River, a pontoon tied to a large wooden dock, garden littered with sculptures of angels, barbecue the size of a hot dog cart.

"Oops, love. Lunch?" William asked, belly hanging over beige khaki shorts like a bowling ball, face crumpled with fatigue. He'd worked another sixty-hour week and had gone in again this morning. I got up and walked to the house. In the kitchen, I opened a can of chicken noodle soup, emptied the contents into a pot, added water, and then made tuna fish sandwiches.

"Milk?" I asked.

We ate lunch on the patio. William chewed noisily. I chewed quietly. We'd been a mismatch from the start. I married him because he seemed sensible. His work at the bank promised us a nice home and a quiet, stable life. I didn't get that growing up in Gogama with all those brothers, a loud father, and a mother who was always at bingo.

What had attracted me at first was William's devotion. It didn't take long for it to become irritating. He doted on me, plain old plump me. Of course he noticed Pauline. She was a sexy twenty-something with long legs, on full display in tight jean shorts, balanced over a pair of wedge-heeled shoes. He'd said he'd never seen such beautiful legs on a woman. It just got better as the eye travelled up the leg, he'd said, referring to her thin waist, pert tits, large blue eyes, and blonde hair in a quasi-beehive. She had a tattoo on her arm of a fifties vintage guitar with a blonde pin-up in a red bathing suit and heels clinging around the neck. Look was all he'd do.

He gave me a peck on the cheek, breath smelling of tuna, and left a smear of mayonnaise on my face. I brushed it off on a napkin. He was talking, I was half-listening. John was outside and I could hear him whistling. He liked fifties music. The song was slow and sexy. I didn't know the name. What did I know about anything cool?

"What do you think?" William asked.

"That's fine," I said.

He'd been talking about going to Cuba after he finished his quarter-end reports. I wasn't interested. Another week-long stay at an all-inclusive resort with travellers who smoked wherever they wanted, carried steel Bubba cups filled with rum, gorged themselves at the buffet, and generally had nothing interesting to say had very little appeal to me.

John took Pauline to Tennessee in May. They went to the Grand Ole Opry, toured Graceland, and drove through Memphis on the day B.B. King died. Year before, they went to Texas, took the interstate through Houston. John told me the roadside rivers were swollen, and an hour later, after they left the city, the highway they'd just driven on was washed out due to flooding. They were driving straight into a hurricane in southwestern Louisiana, but he wasn't afraid; he just kept driving.

William washed our dishes, wiped the counters, taking care to get every crumb, and took out the recycling. All the while talking excitedly about the pool at the resort he'd decided on and which of the four restaurants we'd have fancy dinner in. Japanese or Italian? It didn't matter to me. I had nothing to say on the subject. I stopped listening. John's singing was all I wanted to hear.

HE SANG SOFTLY WHILE strumming blues riffs on his powder blue vintage guitar. He and Pauline had only been living beside us for a few months. I'd brought cake over to welcome Pauline at Easter and she'd said little more than, Thanks babe, before lighting a cigarette and bowing her head to continue texting a friend. I didn't bother to visit again. But one night in May, when the evenings were getting warmer, John came out to play on his patio. I heard him and stopped taking clothes off the line. I smiled and clapped.

"Hey, come join me for a beer," he said.

I nodded and took the basket of clothes in the house. I'd made a raspberry jelly roll for William earlier in the day. I cut two large pieces and carried the plate next door.

He offered me a Corona with a lime lodged in the bottle's neck.

"Where's Pauline?"

"Out at a bar with the girls from work. I'd rather play than listen to that electronic music."

"You play so well," I said.

"Thanks. Want to find people to play with but I've been too busy."

And he had been. I'd watched him settling in, repairing things on the house, fixing up the garden. She left for work in the mornings and didn't come home again until three or four a.m. He held up a book of essays on B.B. King he'd started reading. Did I know that blues lyrics warn against forbidden impulses, gratify these impulses in fantasy, and then symbolically punish?

"Say that again," I said guzzling my beer, hoping he wouldn't see what impulses I was hoping for the willpower not to gratify. He picked up the jelly roll, tracing the outer layers of the coil with his tongue to gather the raspberry jam.

"Your lips are pink," I whispered.

He stuck his tongue in the centre and sucked the rest of the jam out and wiped his mouth with the back of his hand and winked.

"I'll get more jelly roll," I said.

When I returned, he was strumming the chords for a song he told me was called "Man Stealer Blues" by Bessie Jackson. About a woman who'd lost her man and can't sleep because she isn't used to sleeping by herself. I pictured him lying in bed alone. And then I pictured me slipping in beside him.

The evening was growing dark. The moon had appeared and its reflection on the lake seemed like the silvery underside of a dead fish, bloated and floating on the surface. The mid-May air had turned chilly.

"Speaking of bed, I must go myself," I said. I walked back to my yard, looking over my shoulder. He put his guitar in its case before carrying it inside. He was mesmerizing when he played.

I wanted to kiss him goodnight, but I reined in the impulse. I felt a pang of guilt about William. I'd let John eat all of his jelly roll.

AFTER WE'D EATEN TUNA sandwiches and soup, William brought me a glass of lemonade. He'd squeezed the lemons himself, added a teaspoon of sugar and a sprig of mint.

"Thanks," I said.

I went to the kitchen to stuff a plastic bag full of crackers and to pour the rest of the lemonade into a thermos. Twenty minutes later the pontoon was moving along a narrow section of river. The shores were lush with mottled birch trees. The rock cliffs on either side were a dusty peach with black rings of shale. William pointed to a bird. I could barely see it, so I raised my hand above my brow to block the sheath of sun. I finally saw it when William nudged me with his elbow — white and scabby with the psoriasis he'd had since adolescence — and hooted with joy at witnessing such a fine bird. The heron stood daintily on one leg the width of a drinking straw. As the boat swayed in the mild current, the bird swooped upwards with one ferocious flap of its blue wings.

That is why William loved living here. To be close to marvels such as this. He found aquatic life and waterfowl fascinating. I was bored. My dolt of a husband was craning his neck to watch a stupid bird take flight. I wanted to get out of the boat and float on my own, but the lake was full of snakes. There was no getting out. William and the boat would not drift away from me.

He tried to engage me, told a story about a man in his office who'd bought his wife two peach-faced lovebirds. I was certain that he was hinting, wanting permission to bring caged birds in the house.

"We have enough already," I muttered, hoping he'd catch my snide hint. I felt like a caged bird.

"Yes. Just us lovebirds," he said and smiled.

I stifled the urge to yell. How could he not see how bored I was? How meaningless my days? With all the dreary housework I already did, he wanted me cleaning birdcages too? I woke up the other morning and the pile of laundry, hand towels and socks piled over William's white work undershirts looked like a marble bust. A sock for a long Roman nose, a white shirt for the marble skin, a hand towel for a tunic. I must have been over-tired to see such sculpture in a pile of clothes to be folded, but it looked like the Roman hero Caesar, who'd conquered Gaul, forever memorialized in stone.

My life paled in comparison. All I did was contribute to William's work life: cleaning his clothes, stocking the fridge, keeping his toothbrush upright in the holder so it wouldn't breed germs. I wanted an adventure, not a dreary office job, but something exciting. Sex was the something that would dissipate the dullness. Pauline had this with another man. I wanted to have what she had no use for.

After William docked the boat and helped me ashore, I made a light supper. William sat at the small desk in the corner and turned on the laptop. He'd be immersed in his online newspapers until midnight or so. Then he'd fall asleep on the couch, the sports network blaring, until I came downstairs at two in the morning, nudged him awake and told him to come to bed.

THE DAY I SPOTTED Pauline with the other man, John was fishing on Crooked Lake. She didn't work on Saturday morning. She got up that day at noon, draped a towel over the patio rail and lay naked on her lounger. A pile of empty beer cans at her feet next to the iPod in a speaker stand. The irritating electronic music she played drove me nuts. I sat by myself in my kitchen, clutching a mug of tea, trying to hear my own radio, wondering whether I should ask her to turn it down. I got up and parted the kitchen curtains. It faced the driveway we shared. A car pulled up and her other man got out. She rolled over and waved.

He sat next to her and put his hands on her breasts. She kissed him and he pulled her through the patio door, into the house, and closed the curtains.

I felt like I could write my own blues lyric now. Something akin to "that woman don't love that man, let me love him if I can." I was gleeful. Wicked of me to derive such a sense of gain from what I'd witnessed, but I felt as if the power her manoeuver gave me was limitless.

I spent the afternoon watching blues videos on YouTube.

They emerged, dishevelled and giddy, when a few more of Pauline's friends showed up. They roasted corn, grilled burgers, and drank Molson Canadians until I fell asleep with bright orange plugs in my ears.

ON MONDAY MORNING I looked outside for John. He was at the dock with his shirt off. Skin bronzed as a pecan. I primped in the powder room mirror, adding lip gloss and second-guessing my outfit. I went upstairs to find the most revealing thing I owned: a white tank top I'd bought the year I married. I remember wearing it on a warm afternoon when we first bought the pontoon. It fit then. And I was blissful, out on the lake, proud of my new home. I couldn't even pull it down past my waist now.

I took it off and put on William's Old Navy T-shirt. It was loose and hid the flab around my waist. I went downstairs. Took great care to make John coffee, added a splash of vanilla flavoured cream.

"Beautiful day," John said.

"Coffee?" I asked and handed him a cup.

"You make the best coffee around," he said and told me he had a job interview the next morning.

"Organizing my tackle box helps my nerves," he said. "Stupid, eh?"

"Not at all."

He showed me his collection of fishing tackle: rainbow-coloured feathers with weighted baubles, sparkly rubber fish with vicious hooks hidden amongst thin, squid-like tentacles.

"How do you put it on the rod?" I asked.

He put his hands over mine and guided the line through. I quivered under the warmth of his hands. I wanted to do something declarative. Foolish. Impulsive. Clasp his hand to my heart and sigh. But the moment went by. His arms lay on mine as he led me through the art of casting a line. I wondered if he could feel how hot I'd become. How fast my heart was beating. I gave him the rod and he reeled the line back in. He collected his tackle and told me he'd better get going, time to get Pauline up and make breakfast.

I didn't see him for two days.

"How did the interview go?"

"Guy was a jerk. Not my thing anyway."

John sold cars; he owned a vintage Cadillac when they lived in Parry Sound, but sold it to help them move to Sudbury so Pauline could work at the dental office.

"He wanted me to sell tractors. What do I know about tractors?" John said.

"Any of the dealerships in town hiring?"

He shook his head, "EI's gonna run out soon."

"You'll find something," I said.

In the meantime, he was quite content to load up his truck for some time in the woods. If he was going to be away for a few days, Pauline's man would certainly be over.

"I need to tell you something about Pauline," I said.

"Don't need to hear nothing about Pauline," John said.

"But she's —"

"My wife."

I was disappointed that he didn't want to hear. He didn't want to see her for what she was. And what could I say anyway? What could I tell John? That a man came over and cupped his wife's tits while he was away? I didn't know what went on behind closed doors. For all I knew they had an open marriage. Sure as hell explained the time he spent with me.

"I should get home," I said.

"I'm out at the lake for the next few days. Want me to catch a few fish for you?"

Nothing I liked better than fresh fish. John always brought me back something after his time in the woods. He once brought me two plump pickerel. I filleted them right out on the picnic table, cut out the pulsing innards and threw them in the grass for the racoons. I grilled them on the barbecue and ate them before William came home.

As I turned to go, Pauline drove up in the pickup truck. She slammed on the brakes and pummelled the plastic garbage bins in the driveway. Her forehead bumped the steering wheel and she sat blinking and staring over the dashboard. She smiled toward an unseen audience of yokels that could appreciate the hilarity of reckless driving.

"What are you starin' at, Oops? An old girl like you will not attract a man like John, so don't even think about it," Pauline said.

I hung my head and walked inside. I settled down that night with a novel. I hoped the noise next door would stop at a decent hour, but it didn't. The next morning I was up earlier than usual. Off to town to shop. Hours later I pulled the car in the driveway. Some T-shirts and shorts for William, kitchen towels, new salt and pepper mills, and gardening tools in bags beside me on the seat. Despite the morning spent at the New Sudbury Centre I couldn't shake the feeling of listlessness. Or was it uselessness? Another lonely summer loomed ahead — an enclosed tunnel, no way out but through. All my friends had jobs or children. I had neither. No matter how hard we'd tried, we'd never conceived. No one was hiring in town. With William at work all the time, the only fulfilling moments I had were when I spent time with John. Or hoped to spend time with him.

I changed into my bathing suit and went to the dock. I dove in. When I surfaced, a grey suv had pulled in the driveway. It was Pauline's other man. He got out of the car, handsome and clean cut in a baby blue polo shirt and khaki pants. His sleek blonde hair shone. Pauline came out of the house and yelled Blake. Blake? John had mentioned that was the name of the owner of the tractor dealership. So that was why he didn't get the job. The pair of snakes.

WHEN HE GOT BACK from his time in the woods, we sat on his patio and he sang a blues song about a woman who loves everybody else except her man. There was anguish in John's eyes.

It was unbearable to witness. I wanted to hold him, wash away his sorrow, and kiss him until he laughed. Make him as happy as he made me. Just being in his presence, listening to him sing, evoked such contentment that I didn't want our time together to end.

He'd been reading another essay from the B.B. King book and according to it there was meaning associated with the tempo of a blues song. If the singer turned their aggression inward they wrote a masochistic, self-pitying, slow blues song. And then he sang something he'd written. A song that proclaimed his love for her and his desire for her to treat him right.

I looked down and saw how thick the bones in my knees were, the flesh of my thighs squeezing out of my cut-off shorts. Of course he was thinking about her, singing songs for her, I wondered if it even mattered who was listening. I needed to tell him, I wanted him to stop idolizing her. I told myself that he should know. Now.

"But she's ..."

"Don't muddy the waters," he said.

I sat back. There was nothing I could say. What could I do? He loved her. Not me. Pauline's car pulled up. I jumped. She'd arrived earlier than expected — or was it that late already? Had John and I been sitting on the patio longer than we thought?

"Oops ... am I interrupting?" Pauline said and, climbing the stairs, staggered against the railing. She reached out to remove her pink panties from the line, dropped them and fell laughing.

"You didn't pick up any groceries this week," John said.

"Have a Hungry Man entrée," she said and flung a lacy thong at him.

I stood up to go — no one noticed — looking back as she bumped into the glass patio door, John on his feet soothing and guiding her inside, the weight of her on his shoulder.

"Thanks babe," she said.

"BABE," SHE CALLED OUT the afternoon Blake drove up. I had just surfaced after a dive, sun glistening off the water, splintering vision so I couldn't see the house. I heard her, hooting and hollering, speech slurred. I was sure she'd been drinking all afternoon.

I woke up on the dock an hour later. I'd fallen asleep in the sun. My arms and legs were burned. I moved as slowly as a walrus, hoisted myself to my feet, wincing with pain. At that moment John pulled up in his truck. The suv was gone. Pauline, drunk and talking to herself, sat under the patio umbrella. Smoke from her cigarette circled around her wild hair. Crushed cans of Labatt Blue lay under her wedge heels. John walked into the house without a word. I immersed my feet in the water, cool temperature soothed scorched flesh.

John came back out of the house and shouted, "The house is a mess. Dinner's stuck to the pan."

Pauline giggled and blew smoke in his face.

And then he slapped her.

Pauline sat for a split second in silence, her face lopsided from the blow. She stood up, flicked her cigarette, raised a clenched fist and punched him in the chest. John went inside the house and locked the patio door. Pauline ran around to the front door, but he'd beaten her to it. She pounded on the windows and doors yelling, "Let me in you bastard" and "Open the godamn doors."

"I'll kill you if you come in here," John said.

I lowered myself in the water and hoped I wouldn't be seen. I hovered under the dock, watched between the cracks in the wood. There was no sign of the fight next door relenting.

Twenty minutes later, Pauline, exhausted from yelling, gave up and walked down the street, stumbling on wedge heels, adjusting bra-straps every few feet. I hauled myself out of the water and approached the house.

"Get an eyeful?" John said.

I walked past without a word, heavy-hearted; this was too much. I felt afraid of him. He'd hit her. I wondered why he didn't leave her, untangle himself from this thorny relationship, and come to someone who could really love him.

Later that night, alone in my room, all quiet next door, I fell asleep listening to the CBC. At four in the morning I awoke to hear what at first I mistook for William's television, but was really a car door closing. I didn't dare turn on the light. I crawled across my bed and looked out. My second-floor bedroom window open, moonlight washing the backyard blue, stars strewn across black sky, and the lingering heat of yesterday's sun — or was it the approaching warmth of tomorrow? — thickened the room.

It was John, in his backyard, loading his rod and rifle in the truck for his stay in the woods. Grimness had set in his face, a hardness that drained the zest from his usual sexy half-smile and easy swagger. John glanced up at my window and I moved aside.

A few hours later, William got up off the sofa. I heard his

electric razor, footsteps on the stairs, the range fan as he cooked bacon and eggs for breakfast. He'd leave in thirty minutes. I waited in bed until he was gone.

I knew John was gone. I didn't want to see anyone today. I wanted to take the pontoon out by myself, find a secluded bay and eat, dip my feet in the water, and read. Seeing him slap her reminded me of what my brother did to me years ago. But I didn't want to think about it now. I wanted to be free of worry, relax on the lake.

It had rained overnight. The gravel driveway that separated our properties was pocked with mud puddles. So was the path to the pontoon. I walked down to the dock, balanced on the tips of my toes. The flowers in our gardens stood with petals splayed toward the sun, perky even after a battering from the rain.

I heard a car pull up. Blake behind the wheel. Pauline, still wearing last night's clothes, got out of the car. She bent down and picked up a stone angel from my garden. What was she thinking, entering my garden, taking my angel? What did she want with it? I was about to tell her to put my garden ornament down when she bolted to the glass patio door and raised her hand. Blake held her back; he'd checked the front door. It was open. Pauline threw the angel into my yard.

I ran up the path and picked up the angel. It was heavy, but scrawny Pauline hadn't flinched with the weight of it. I looked around for her, angry, but she'd gone inside. I placed the angel where it belonged next to the flowerbeds, and then walked back down to the dock, as far away as I could from the commotion that I was certain would erupt.

I watched from afar as Blake hauled a suitcase to the car.

Shortly after, Pauline tottered out on heels with a large houseplant in her arms. Its dilapidated leaves, brown and curled, were as big as hubcaps. She struggled to get it in the suv, wedged it in the back seat, folding its leaves to fit inside. There wasn't enough room. Pauline swore. I crouched in the pontoon. Pauline hauled the houseplant out and threw it to the ground. She kicked it. Sank to her knees and pounded it mercilessly. Blake raised her to her feet and stroked her nose gently. He plied her cheeks with small kisses. She squirmed playfully in his embrace. He gestured toward the house. He had her top off before they were inside.

A few minutes later, John's truck pulled up beside Blake's vehicle.

He took his hunting rifle from the back of the truck.

I yelled his name, tripped over the cushions on the floor of the pontoon as I ran toward him. He'd already gone inside. I stopped. The shouts I expected to hear didn't come. Only the roar of one crisp bang.

WHEN HE SLAPPED PAULINE across the face yesterday all the interest I had in John should have withered. As much as I couldn't stand Pauline, he'd hit her. Across the face. In his backyard. In plain view. But his actions seemed to fall in the middle on the spectrum between William's docility and my brutish brothers' severity. I excused it. What does Oprah say about girls who grow up with sexual violence? They either escape it entirely or are attracted to it. What would Oprah say about a girl who managed to do both?

I WAS SIXTEEN. WE were boating on Minisinakwa Lake and I needed to go to the bathroom.

"Not in the latrine. We'll have to clean it," said my oldest brother.

"Will you stop the boat and let me jump out for a minute? Wait for me?"

"Yes, go on," he said.

I jumped in one-hundred-and-sixty-foot-deep water. It felt sharp against my legs and cold against my chest. I struggled to keep my head above. As the warm urine collected around me, I watched the boat speed off, leaving me to fight its wake. "They'll stop now," I whispered aloud. But they hadn't stopped. I treaded water as the boat slunk further away. They aren't going to stop.

I looked around; the shores on either side were more than two hundred feet away. Thoughts of water snakes flicked in my mind. The cold current filtered between my thighs. They still haven't stopped, I said aloud to myself, and adrenalin shot through my thin limbs.

"Dear God, help me," I cried to the hot sun. I lost sight of the boat. I saw one of my father's friends on the south shore, rod by his side, a container of bait held upright in his hands. He found a rock, sat down and prepared his rod.

I shouted his name. He looked up and waved.

"Help me," I shouted.

"Don't panic. I'm coming."

He removed shoes and track pants, pulled off a T-shirt to reveal an undershirt that read Fishing and Beer. Nothing Else Matters. He dove into the lake and swam out to me.

"Can you swim?" he asked, treading water beside me.

"Yes, but I'm afraid to move — the snakes."

"Put your arms around my neck. I'll bring you in," he said. He swam gently back to shore. My panic subsided as he glided, arms and legs pulsing the water, propelling us back to shore. He hoisted me out of the water, wrapped me up in his shirt and asked why I was in the water alone. I pointed at the boat, coming back around the bend in the river. He frowned as the boat stopped, waves chopping at the rocky bank.

"Turned around for you," my brother said.

"Wanted to stay out for the afternoon," another one said.

I cursed my brothers. You left me in the water alone, I thought. But how could I make them understand my terror? How could they, all steel balls and iron fists, understand my feelings? They'd mock me. Call me weak. Why did they tell me they would wait for me and then not?

"Do you want me to walk you home?" my father's friend asked.

"No. I'm fine," I said and hoped the moistness in my eyes would be mistaken for lake water.

When I got back to our house, I had to get past one of my brothers who stood in front of the door. Underneath the borrowed shirt my halter top was askew, one breast scrunched up, its nipple exposed. He walked toward me, mesmerized, cupped my breast, and rubbed his other hand on his shorts. I batted his hand away from me and kicked him. I couldn't get him off. He groaned and semen dripped down his leg. I stiffened in horror at what he'd done. He revolted me, the pickle juice smell of him, wild eyes and open mouth making little mewing noises. I pushed him aside, weeds clinging to my legs, and ran through the door. I threw up in the front hall. "Clean that up, you fuck," my brother yelled at me.

"FUCKERS," I HEARD JOHN say after the crisp bang, the sound of the gunshot that came from inside the house. He came out carrying the rifle. He was wearing a plaid hunter's jacket. He sat on a patio chair. He lit a cigarette.

"Out fishing yesterday, looked up to see a bull moose swimming toward me, fast. As if I was in his territory. Got him with one clean shot."

"Please. Tell me. Tell me you didn't, did you?" My hands shook as I spoke. I thought I was yelling. But my voice was hoarse, my throat was dry.

"Two of them rutting in my bed," John said. Wisps of smoke rose above his head. He sat, both feet firmly on the floor, chest heaving. Utterly unapologetic.

I didn't want to be next to him. He couldn't have. No. Impossible. This wouldn't, couldn't happen in our neighbourhood. He wouldn't have gone that far; it was only a slap. Once. Were they, could they be, alive in there, crawling on the floor in pools of blood, tending to one another's wounds? Where exactly had he wounded them? Arms?, Legs? Hands? Hearts? If they weren't crawling around in there, they'd be dead, one on top of the other. Was Blake still inside of her?

THE AIR SMELLED RANK. John stank of campfire, smoke, wet dog fur, and coppery lake water.

The flashing lights of the police car bathed our houses in scarlet. When they turned into the driveway, crushing Pauline's house-plant, I'd already limped back to my house and closed the door. Behind the curtain in the kitchen window, fabric held back with trembling fingers, I watched John surrender and raise his hands to the officer who'd taken his rifle. Within minutes, Pauline and Blake were escorted out of the house. John had shot out the bedroom window — or so I'd learned later from the neighbour across the street. She'd heard the gun and called the police.

I closed the curtain. I'd seen enough. *William.* I need William.

I called him. Stuck behind a stopped train on the north side of the tracks, he told me not to cry. Not to get in the car. To lock the door and stay away from the windows in case the media showed up. I sank to the floor. I couldn't stop hearing the siren, the noise of the officers. I was haunted by the memory of the single gunshot. Why didn't I tell John? Why didn't I say something? I could have moved faster. I could have prevented him from going inside the house and getting himself in trouble by firing the gun, attempting — what? What exactly had he planned on doing?

I made a cup of tea and sat down on the sofa. I sat there all afternoon, ignoring the officers knocking on my door. I'd have to talk to them sooner or later. But I couldn't move. A little bird, a chimney swift to be precise — I recalled William telling me about them — sang out, announcing sunset. Even though my hands were shaking, I took care to prepare William's favourite, macaroni and cheese, for supper. When he came home he held me for a long time, told me we'd need to talk to the police, but thank God I was safe. He would book us that getaway in Cuba. We'd leave as soon as this was over. There was a shallow cove he knew I'd like. He'd looked at it on Trip Advisor. It was a haven for tropical fish. We'll see all sorts, he said. I pictured the vivid colours, raincoat yellow and crayon blue on the flat-faced, thin fish I didn't know the name of.

When the macaroni was in the oven, we went outside to face the police. After a few questions — had this happened before, did we see any other violence, did they fight often, and I said in my sincerest voice, that I never saw them fight, they were as quiet as church mice — they were done with me. For now, the cop said as we turned towards our house. We went back inside. William ate noisily. I didn't snarl at him.

After dinner we shared a pot of tea and he read the papers online. The story already dominated the news. William read passages from the stories, condemnations on Twitter from colleagues, Pauline's family and friends, and ludicrous quotes from neighbours who said they knew all along something like this would happen to that loud couple down the street with the gorgeous house that overlooked the lake.

The next morning, I woke up on the sofa to the radio, the host on News Talk discussing domestic violence on the banks of the Wanapitei. I snuck outside to avoid William.

An ashen pallor had descended on John's property. I ran to the pontoon. I shook as I stepped in the boat and started the motor. I looked up to see William watching me through the window. I turned away. I needed to do this. Unexpectedly overwhelmed, a surge of tears began to flow. I felt ashamed of how much I'd longed for his body, how mesmerized I was by his eyes and that hair, the contours of his chest and arms. How easily I'd been seduced by the way he sang and spoke about music and the way he played guitar.

An hour later I docked the pontoon. And, for the first time in almost a year, it was quiet on our street. But my ears rang. If the heat that rose from the rocks in sizzling waves made noise it would sound like what was swirling in my head.

Another bird William had pointed out, a grackle, landed on the patio. It let loose a garbled shriek. I thought of its purpose, here at this moment in my backyard. Would it plunder a seed from the garden, claw a worm from the soil? Or would it leave something behind? Perhaps scatter some seeds from its droppings that would introduce a new type of flower. The bird lifted itself up on a sharp angle, and landed on top of the evergreen tree across the lake.

I thought of those nights we'd spent on the patio when he told me all he'd learned about blues music. I wish I'd taken heed when he'd said if aggression is turned outward blues lyricists write a sadistic and obscene fast blues song. I'd been impressed, amazed that all of those messages could be contained in one style of music. But I should have known that he already knew when he sang that song about the blues falling down like rain and how the sadness was so deep it made him feel that his life was like water swirling down the drain. I wondered if he'd wanted to kill them then, but in the last minute changed his mind. If he'd intended to kill her when he took the rifle from the back of the truck, he must have sensed there was something worth living for, something bigger than the whole situation, and simply shot out the window to scare her. I'd never know. They left that day and never came back. He was sentenced to three years in prison and she went home to Parry Sound to live with her mother, as I heard from the vine of gossip that sprouted on my street and spread throughout town.

I caught my reflection in the glass patio door and it confirmed what I already knew but had tried to hide. I saw what Pauline had laughed at. The frumpy woman before my eyes could not have made someone half her age feel threatened, even if she had tried. I'd been so desperate for my fantasies to come true I hadn't considered how heartbroken, deeply in love, and subsequently betrayed John must have felt.

I went back inside and settled on the couch, wrapped myself in a blanket. Even though the room was hot, I shivered. The chain on the ceiling fan snapped as it spun on high speed. Hours later I woke up to William stroking my cheek. I'd kicked the blanket off myself while sleeping. William ushered me to bed and steadied me on the stairs. Before dawn, half-asleep, I called out his name. His warm hand found my waist. I squeezed his arm. In the half-light, I sensed the obvious. In my unassuming husband's gentle embrace, a sense of relief took root.

# A Duck to Water

WIND-RUMPLED WATER, RESEMBLING plucked avian flesh, stirred on the River Seine. Christophe held Emma's hand as they walked down the concrete stairs, freckled with green moss, to the banks of the river.

Emma shivered.

"You've got goosebumps," Christophe said, gathering her in his arms.

"A chill," Emma said, and tried to hide her worry. They were meeting Christophe's daughter Sistine for drinks later. It would be the first time Emma and the twenty-nine-year-old art historian would meet. How could she, a forty-eight-year-old Canadian, impress Sistine? Had Sistine ever gotten over the death of her mother? A famous television journalist on assignment in Moscow, covering the collapse of the Soviet Union in 1991. Her plane had crashed thirty minutes after takeoff. The funeral procession in Paris drew thousands. Mourners converged along the Champs-Élysées prostrate with grief, bearing witness to the life of a beloved national treasure.

Emma pointed to a large mallard, mottled brown feathers bristling as she waddled toward the water, six ducklings following behind. The bird dove into the river, surfaced, twitched her neck, and jabbed the water with her beak.

Christophe had just read a book on Gallo-Roman mythology. The cover pictured the goddess of the River Seine standing on a boat shaped like a duck. One of the things he had learned was that the people of Gaul under imperial Rome believed waterfowl to symbolise transition because of their migration patterns.

"They winter in France and return to their breeding grounds in spring," Christophe said.

Emma shuddered. Female ducks endure monstrous assault from groups of competing males, vying for them during breeding season. Frequently, they drown. Yet this hen, who'd somehow managed to survive, strode valiantly across the river; her delicate ducklings in a line behind. Emma wouldn't know what to do with a child of her own, let alone a raft the size of that.

He was almost ten years older than she and, even though streaks of grey snaked through his widow's peak, his sorbet-white skin, bright eyes, and generous mouth made him appear youthful. He pulled two ham-and-cheese baguettes from his bag. The salt of thinly shaved ham dissolved in their mouths. He poured café au lait from a thermos and they shared the steel cup.

"I'd like to bring you to Marseille this weekend," he said.

Emma nodded. She wanted to go. She was falling in love with him. These feelings had caught her by surprise. They'd only started dating in October. At the Frankfurt Book Fair, Christophe, the Paris-based publisher of Byzantine Books, had dropped by her booth. He told her later that it wasn't the cover of the book she was promoting, blown up and mounted on a banner, but Emma herself, with those gorgeous long legs and wide smile, who'd captured his attention. Emma, the marketing director for a mid-size Canadian publisher, had sold the rights to their *Hip-Hop Mother Goose* book to twelve publishers. She was ecstatic. He invited her for a celebratory toast at the hotel. After the other publishers and staff had trickled off to bed, Christophe and Emma talked in the bar until morning. Although Emma had known about him for most of her professional life, knew of his publishing successes and failures — and always well aware of the female company he'd kept — this was the first time they'd spent any personal time together. She discovered that Christophe played the piano. He loved to travel. Favoured checkerboard socks over plain ones. Hated espresso, loved crisp white sheets and American jazz, and was allergic to dogs. They shared a mutual love of pistachios. She told him about leaving Halifax to study publishing in Toronto.

"I missed the Atlantic Ocean so much I'd sit at Queen's Quay and watch the boats in the harbour every day after work."

"Why didn't you go back?"

"My father was a fisherman from Newfoundland. He always told me to stay where the work was."

Christophe's father was also a fisherman. He'd left his other sons the fishing fleet, but Christophe had inherited the houseboat.

"RED OR WHITE?" SISTINE asked, translating for the waiter on the terrace of Chez Julien.

Emma responded to the waiter in French.

"You speak French," Sistine said.

"My mother is Acadian."

Sistine looked at her and nodded in approval. The smell of bread and broth and red wine rich. Sistine, distracted by the comings and goings of friends who stopped by the table to converse and envelop Christophe in hugs, didn't have much left to say to Emma. Listening intently, Emma realized that she didn't speak, or understand, French much at all. What she had managed to catch, after piecing together snatches of conversation, was that Sistine had said that she figured Emma was just another one of her father's lame ducks, with a successor, another woman, perhaps younger and French, waiting just around the corner. Everyone at the table had laughed and Christophe shook his head and scolded Sistine.

By evening's end Sistine jumped up, kissed Emma and Christophe on both cheeks, jumped on her moped, and went back to her apartment. Emma felt like she hadn't gotten to know a thing about Sistine.

"Don't worry, she likes you," Christophe said.

ON THE TRAIN FROM Paris to Marseille they sped past vineyards in Côte d'Or. The squat vines, branches curling under a plume of dark leaves, cocooned ripe grapes. The chalky tips of the French Alps glistened under the amber sun.

"The highest peak is Mont Blanc. It's over fifteen thousand feet," Christophe said.

"Why aren't you a professor?"

"I like to read and to share facts, but I can't bear speaking in front of people."

Emma couldn't either. Her parents had begged her to get a doctorate after her master's. She didn't want to. All she wanted to do was make books. But she enrolled anyway, endured a year at Dalhousie, then dropped out to take the publishing program at a college in Toronto.

The train pulled into the Gare de Marseille-Saint-Charles. They wheeled their suitcases through sloping cobbled alleyways, where lean men with dark eyes smoked cigarettes. Through the crowd of cars and city buses they arrived in Vieux Port. Sailboats crowded the harbour; masts, like over-sized fishing poles, scraped the sky.

"Which one's yours?"

"Right here," Christophe said, as he helped her aboard the houseboat. A quaint thing, with two beds and a kitchenette, handmade blue-and-white curtains on windows, jars of spices lining the counters. Christophe turned on the motor and they set out on the turquoise sea. On shore, Emma saw an old man, cap askew, cast a fishing line from a cove in the taupe rocks. They passed an abandoned prison on an island as Marseille shrank from view.

In the open expanse of the Mediterranean, an unexpected sweet melon scent floated in the air around them. Without so much as a comment or hint, Emma took off her tank top and shorts and jumped into the water. Christophe followed, diving in, surfacing beside her. Emma was surprised by the buoyancy she was experiencing. This was nothing like the Atlantic Ocean she knew so well. Side by side, they floated on their backs, the salt water lapping over their thighs and stomachs. A deep sense of calm settled over Emma. She'd never felt so happy. The sun was bright, the water was warm, and she was in love. Christophe turned on his stomach and swam to the boat's ladder. He climbed up effortlessly.

"Hungry?" he called from the deck.

Emma swam to the boat and climbed up. Christophe handed her a glass of wine as soon as she'd dried herself. "Put on lots of sun block and stay here. I'm going to the galley." With that, he disappeared into the cabin

Emma saturated her skin with lotion, sipped her wine, and fell asleep. She hadn't slept too long before the sound of Christophe setting up a supper on the deck woke her. Over a plate of grilled fish and peppers he talked about his life in Paris and how, since his wife had died, he had dated a lot of women but no one had captured his heart. Until now. He wondered if, well, if she'd …

"Marry you?"

"Why not? Come live with me in Paris."

He pulled his hair from his forehead and his eyebrows shot up in expectation as he waited for her response. Her life had been focussed exclusively on her work and her career. Hers was one of those all-consuming jobs that left little room for a personal life. And now, when she'd least expected it, along came love. She wanted nothing more than to marry him.

IN MID-AUGUST CHRISTOPHE AND Sistine arrived in Toronto. Sistine stayed on the pullout couch in the smaller bedroom while Christophe shared Emma's room.

"You'll like my father's house in Noisy-le-Roi," Sistine said, surveying the narrow living space in Emma's Annex area semi-detached bay-and-gable house.

Emma had planned a few outings. The first: a trip to the Art Gallery of Ontario to see the Motherwell exhibit. She met them after work. The dimly-lit room at the gallery was cold. The floors were glossy. There was little dust. In front of the artist's *Je t'aime* series Sistine rolled her eyes.

"Why does this American insist on scrawling French on his paintings?"

Emma gulped.

Sistine wandered ahead, shaking her head in disapproval at the paintings. After the exhibit, Emma suggested they get soft ice cream cones, her favourite, from the truck near Grange Park. "We prefer savoury foods," Sistine said.

"There's a great sushi bar up the street," she said.

In bed with Christophe that evening she asked, "How am I going to win her over?"

"Why don't the two of you go out alone?"

EMMA ASKED SISTINE TO join her for a picnic on Toronto Island. They walked along Queen's Quay and boarded the ferry at Bay Street. The royal blue water sparkled as the ferry crossed.

"Look at that lake freighter. She's over six hundred feet," Emma said and her face lit up.

"Elle est merveilleuse," Sistine said and looked away.

On Ward's Island they walked to the swimming cove. Emma carried a tote bag filled with turkey sandwiches, cubed watermelon, and iced tea. Sistine snapped her gum. Her enormous sunglasses shielded her eyes.

"It's pretty here," she said.

Emma nodded and smiled, relieved that Sistine took to the place. Emma spread a blanket and they sat down. A duck approached and took a crust of bread from Sistine.

"They take what they want here. They're not shy," Sistine said.

The duck waddled toward shore. Emma turned to tell her that she looked forward to moving to France, hoped they'd all be comfortable together, when Sistine, topless, nipples wrinkled and stiff, asked for an iced tea. Emma wanted to bury herself in the sand. An old woman turned her beach chair away. Two young men by the shore removed their sunglasses and pointed.

"Why don't we move to another section of the Island?"

"If you like," Sistine said.

At Hanlan's Point, the nude beach, Sistine got in the water. The heat frustrated Emma, but she did not feel comfortable enough to disrobe. She was unaccustomed to public nudity.

"Hot?" Sistine asked, returning to the blanket.

Emma blushed and nodded as a man beside her dabbed suntan lotion on his scrotum.

"My mom would have liked swimming here," Sistine said.

Emma would not be outdone by the memory of Sistine's mother. She removed her tank top. Her breasts were white as marzipan. She galloped to shore and knelt down in the water. All around her, fit, young nudists, comfortable in their own skin, were oblivious to Emma's discomfort. Emma dreaded emerging. When she returned to the blanket she couldn't find her top.

"You're shy?" Sistine asked.

"No —"

"French customs will take getting used to."

"I'm sure I'll take to France like a duck to water," Emma said.

THE LAST TWO WEEKS of August went by quickly. It had been an exceptionally humid month. Emma had gotten a heat rash on her breasts and thighs. Cream hadn't helped. Powder hadn't soothed. At the coffee machine, she'd told a colleague that she'd wanted to come to work topless. The woman had laughed so much her mug had shaken. And then, before they knew it, Labour Day weekend had arrived.

The wedding ceremony, that Saturday, took place in the Chambers at City Hall, a bright room with blonde oak floors and purple orchids in every corner. Emma wore an A-line white linen dress and birdcage veil, Christophe a black tuxedo, and Sistine a red silk dress. Emma's mother and father had flown in from Halifax, her mother had put flowers on her husband's wheelchair and had dabbed the corners of his eyes with a cotton handkerchief.

The ceremony, quick and non-sentimental, practical and austere, was over before they knew it.

Afterward they brought her parents back to the hotel across the street, ordered steak and lobster through room service and set them up with a movie on HBO. Christophe gathered Emma's hand in his.

"What would you like to eat my love?"
"Ice cream," Emma said.
"Fattening," Sistine said under her breath.
They jumped on the Dundas streetcar. An old woman, face covered by large black cataract sunglasses, congratulated them. At Dundas West station Christophe and Emma, giggling like teenagers, ordered fries from the McDonald's kiosk and ate them on the Junction bus. At the shop Emma ordered spiced plum, Christophe tried a cedar and orange zest-flavoured kind called Muskoka Sun while Sistine picked at her bowl of Quebec blue cheese ice cream. Emma felt a childlike happiness, her husband beside her, dribbles of ice cream spotting the lapel of his tuxedo jacket, not a care in the world. She slid her shoes off under the table and rubbed his legs. Christophe stood up to go to the counter for more.
"Papa, that's too much ice cream," said Sistine.
"Excuse me?"
"You've had enough."
"If we want to have ice cream let us have our goddamn ice cream," Emma said.
"He's not supposed to get old and fat with you," Sistine said and burst into tears.
"*Ma chérie*," said Christophe and sat back down.
"Why don't we take a walk through High Park?"

AT THE SHORES OF Grenadier Pond, with a maple-leaf-shaped flower bed behind her and duck feathers clumped at her feet, Sistine continued to sniffle. She wiped the mascara from her cheeks with one hand and bunched the hem of her red dress in the other.
Emma and Christophe looked at one another in bewilderment.

"I'm sorry. This is not how I wanted to behave at all," Sistine said. She told them it hadn't really sunk in until today. That she liked Emma, really she did, but how could she bear another woman's things in the house on a permanent basis?

"Up until now his girlfriends have only stayed a short while. But you'll be in his, and my childhood home permanently." She didn't know if she could deal with someone playing the role of mother in her life.

"I don't know if I can either," said Emma.

"What?" said Christophe.

"What do I know about being a mother? Nothing. But I know I love your father. Enough to give up everything I know to move to a country I know nothing about," said Emma.

A passenger airplane flew overhead. Emma looked up and wondered if it was coming home or leaving town.

AT THE GATE WAITING for their flight, Christophe received a text from Sistine wishing them a safe flight home. Sistine had left the day after the wedding, excuses made about work commitments. Christophe had wanted to drive her to the airport, but she'd refused.

"She'll come around," Christophe said.

Emma knew that Sistine and Christophe would be all right. Their lives hadn't been uprooted. Their routines would remain intact and they both had meaningful work to occupy their time. Christophe had assured her that she'd be okay too. She could take language classes, explore the city and help him around the office.

The boarding call for their flight was announced. Emma's hands shook. Christophe held one and gently rubbed it with his thumb. Emma tucked a piece of hair behind one ear, rubbed the back of her neck and felt the knot of muscles give. She took a final sip of water, tucked the bottle in her purse, and grabbed her passport.

# *Differential Settlement*

VIRTUE HADN'T EXPECTED NATHANIEL to be so fetching. Standing in front of a group of local business owners in skinny jeans and a striped shirt, his dark curly hair coiled over his forehead, he spoke commandingly. With his handsome nose, heart-shaped face and plump lips, Virtue thought the only word to describe him was *pretty*.

"Last week a bid was put forth at City Council to build a condo in our community," said Nathaniel.

"They must be stopped," said a man who co-owned a bar popular with poets.

"A high-rise will impact my business," said another bar owner.

"This puts all of our businesses at risk," said Nathaniel. He owned the organic ice cream shop.

"They'll try to get us evicted," said Nik, co-owner of a live music and strip bar.

Virtue watched as her best friend, and next-door neighbour, Holly, squirmed as her new boss Gwen, a real estate agent, walked in. She'd taken Holly on as an assistant the month before. Holly had worked for Virginia Johnson, the clothing and housewares designer at College and Dovercourt, before Virginia closed her shop; she was wearing a Virginia Johnson original, a wrap-around dress covered in spring-green and eggplant-purple crocodiles, gorgeous in combination with her Bettie Page-style hair and black cat's-eye glasses. Her apartment looked like Johnson's studio, vibrant, colourful, fresh — covered in swathes of Virginia Johnson fabric, patterned with teal birdcages. These hung from her ceiling, which leaked like all the apartments in the complex. Holly had hoped to continue apprenticing with Virginia and get her own clothing line for toddlers off the ground, but Virginia closed the storefront to focus on online sales. Now Holly was working for Gwen, who sold overpriced houses in the neighbourhood.

"Nathaniel isn't talking sense," said Gwen and stood beside him at the front of the room. "This development invigorates our neighbourhood and stimulates local business."

"They'll raise our property taxes," said a woman who owned the bead-and-craft store.

"I heard taxes are going up as much as a thousand per cent," said the bartender from the craft beer shop.

"It's called 'highest best use' and it's meant to force us to re-locate or to sell to the developers. I have postcards designed to raise community awareness. Please consider displaying them at your business," said Nathaniel.

After coffee and biscotti, the crowd dispersed. On the way out Nathaniel pressed postcards in Virtue's hand and cupped her elbow.

"Hello owner of the Oyster Bar. I've seen you in the business services line at the bank," said Nathaniel.

"At my best when making a deposit," said Virtue.

Outside Holly asked, "What was that all about?"

"Me being ridiculous in front of a guy I think is cute," said Virtue.

Gwen waved and came over.

"I'm giving you my coordinates for tomorrow morning," said Gwen and sent Holly a text.

When Gwen walked away Holly said, "Gwen's having an affair with her business partner's husband."

"And you of all people are covering for her?"

Holly shook her head helplessly. She had met her ex-husband when they were in university. She had a kiosk called Eat your Words: Baked Goods & Books at Ontario Place. She sold used books her mother's friends donated and freshly-baked muffins, cupcakes, cookies, and tarts she'd baked at four a.m. every morning. Her ex-husband had cycled the boardwalk, selling ice cream from a deep freezer trailer attached to his bike. He brought her an ice cream from his cart every day, treated them as if they were bouquets of roses, covered the stick with a napkin before giving her one. They'd married within the year. When she caught him in bed with his Marketing for Small Business professor, she'd felt like nothing else in the world could ever hurt so much.

When Holly moved into the bachelor next door, ten years ago this spring, she found Virtue sitting in the small courtyard reading a magazine. Holly approached with six bottles of beer in an Anthropologie bag; they spent that afternoon drinking, the evening at the Dakota Tavern dancing to bearded bluegrass musicians, and gorging on poutine at the Lakeview Lunch afterward.

"She's put me in a difficult position," said Holly.

"That's sleazy."

"That's Gwen."

Back in her apartment, alone in her bedroom, Virtue stood with one hand raised toward the ceiling. Warm water dripped through the damp plaster and landed in a plastic bucket. The water pipe in the roof was leaking again. The building's caretaker had patched it up months ago, with duct tape. It had leaked countless times before; last spring, she'd moved her mattress out to the living room, set up a sleeping area between an old futon — which she'd since given to a bike courier who lived one floor below — and her mountain bike.

In the kitchen, she turned on the kettle. She prodded an errant chickpea, trapped in the coil element, blackened and shedding ash. It wouldn't move. A thin line of smoke shot up from the orange element. The smoke detector went off. Virtue ran for the broom and waved it in front of the alarm. She'd complained to the landlord, asked to have an exhaust fan installed, but the landlord told her to find another place if she wanted fancy living.

She leaned against the crooked kitchen door frame. She'd complained about that too, the odd way the doors, floors, and roof slanted, and the landlord — a seventy-five-year-old former architect, forced to leave his profession due to allergies to building materials — left her a message, "We live over Garrison Creek. The building suffers differential settlement, if you don't like the fact that there's no way to settle the sand and get things to straighten out, please feel free to move."

How could she move out of her rental in this city? What could she afford in Toronto where hundred-year-old, energy inefficient, semi-detached homes were selling for millions? The most she could reasonably expect, if she wanted something new, would be a five-hundred-square-foot condo with a Juliette balcony, a useless waste of space with not enough room for a potted plant. She'd taken out a small business loan three years ago to open Oyster Bar and was still paying mostly interest, leaving the principle barely touched. A mortgage, if she'd ever qualify for one, and monthly condo fees, now almost as much as rent, seemed impossible to manage.

The next morning, Virtue woke and checked the bucket at the

foot of her bed. It was filled to the rim. She lugged the bucket to the sink and emptied it. A smell of rot and decay rose from the drain. The apartment stank, despite the placement of scented reed diffusers — *Fluffy Towels* — she'd purchased earlier that week from the Ceramic Shack, a store full of high-end, overpriced decorative throw cushions, garlic presses, and heavy rainbow-coloured pots and kettles.

She showered and dressed quickly and locked the front door on her way out. Minutes later, at her restaurant, the oyster shucker slipped her a raw oyster. She ate a few more before inspecting the tables. She ran her finger along the top to feel if there was grease. The restaurant opened for dinner and stayed open until eleven, so she had time to clean the tables thoroughly, then set them. It took her most of what remained of the morning. After lunch, she reviewed the catering orders. Shortly before two a bicycle courier knocked on the door. He took a pint of Honey Lavender ice cream out from a cooler strapped to his bike and handed it to her.

*Are you free this weekend?* The card read.

She blushed from this wave of attention.

The phone rang. She picked it up on the third ring.

"Did you like the ice cream?" asked Nathaniel.

"I haven't tasted it," said Virtue.

"You don't like ice cream?"

"It just arrived."

"Have a drink at The Communist's Daughter with me before you open?"

Inside the former Portuguese snack bar, on the corner of Dundas and Ossington, revitalized as a live music venue, Virtue waited for Nathaniel. The bartender, a solo vocalist backed by a jazz trio, sang as he sliced lemons and mixed Virtue a whiskey sour, then picked up a battered trumpet and performed a perky solo, before he went back behind the bar to continue mixing drinks. Nathaniel walked in.

"Good of you to come out last night," said Nathaniel and sat down.

Virtue couldn't stop looking at a loose curl that flopped over his forehead.

"I wouldn't have missed it," said Virtue.

Nathaniel ordered drinks.

"Live nearby?" he asked as the bartender placed another whiskey sour in front of her.

"Yes. An eighty-year-old building at Dovercourt and College. You?"

"An apartment above the ice cream shop on Ossington."

The conversation quickly turned to halting the development. Everyone she knew on the Ossington strip, at work, at the Business Improvement Area hated condos. Even the people who lived in the new lofts on Dundas — which were technically condos — hated condos. Nathaniel said that his friend, a real estate agent, had told him that most condos had been purchased by foreign nationals as safe places for inevitable political disruption, regime changes, and subsequent seizure of money and property in their homelands. They were also, according to his friend, vessels for cartels, sold to drug lords to launder money.

"You couldn't pay me to buy into that development," said Nathaniel.

After two drinks, he walked her back to the Oyster Bar.

"How long have you lived here?" asked Nathaniel.

"I moved in when I was twenty, almost fifteen years ago, when nobody but rockabilly punks went to the Lakeview Lunch. Then they renovated the Drake Hotel and then the Gladstone. And now people come here in droves for the live music and hot food. It seemed the perfect place to open my restaurant," Virtue said. She hadn't had much competition, but now she was worried about the new one opening on Queen's Quay. Although in a different part of the city, it was twice the size of hers, had laminate floors, an aquarium behind the bar, leather chairs, and exquisite track lighting. The owners had lured the national champion oyster shucker up from Nova Scotia and hired one of the city's best bartenders.

She thought of the months, weeks, and hours it had taken to get her place ready. The time spent with the flooring and tile companies, picking out the right materials for the dining room, kitchen, and washrooms. The work with the plumbers: choosing faucets, sinks, and toilets. And the time spent matching spoons and forks to plates and bowls. It had seemed endless, but she'd been relentless. Everything had to be just right. She'd spent more time on the restaurant than she'd ever spent on her apartment. Put up with living in an old building — the leaks, the soup-like heat in the summer, and paralyzing cold in the winter — just to have a business.

"I've owned the ice cream shop for five years now. Drained my savings to open it. Had to get rid of my old business partner along the way," said Nathaniel.

"What happened?"

"We had different ideas about how to run things. Our supposedly solid relationship was built on nothing but wet sand. I bought him out."

"What caused the rift?"

"He used out-of-date products. He didn't think we had any responsibility toward the community."

"Selfish."

"I'm putting up flyers tomorrow morning protesting the development. Do you want to come?"

Virtue smoothed her grey cotton dress, a shapeless piece of fabric she hadn't bothered to accessorize, and tucked a strand of hair in the messy bun on top of her head. He put his hands in the back pockets of his skinny jeans. Virtue wanted to touch him.

"Yes. This is such an important issue for our community. I'd love to help you raise awareness," she said.

The next morning, Virtue woke up and emptied the water bucket. She emptied the stale water out of the kettle. The drain gurgled and spit rice grains to the surface. *Not again*, she thought. She finished a cup of tea, gathered her dirty clothes and made her way to the laundry room. In the hallway, the caretaker, a Portuguese man with a baseball cap smudged with grease, poked his head up out of a giant hole in the floor. He wore a flashlight tied to a visor, the light illuminating crusty pipes in the foundation, blackened with a crud that looked like the burnt chickpea remnant in her coil stove.

"Boiler's out again," he said. Last February, in minus twenty-eight degrees Celsius, they hadn't had heat for twelve days. Virtue slept in her winter jacket, turned the oven on broil and kept its door open all night. She didn't know if she could bear another episode. She went back upstairs and banged on the wall above the sink. Holly, in the bachelor apartment next door, thumped back. One thump meant, Are you home? Two thumps meant, Yes, come over. By the time the kettle whistled Holly was at the front door. Inside, seated at the kitchen table, Holly smeared almond butter on bread Virtue had brought home from work.

"Nathaniel sounds great," said Holly. "He's so committed."

Holly's eyes narrowed as she talked about the pending development. She said the word *condo* as if it were a disease. "Blights on the landscape. Those towers down by the lake crowd out the harbour. They are situated on artificial land. They packed the shore of Lake Ontario with landfill. That means anything they could find, including garbage. If living over Garrison Creek has been bad, I don't want to see what the next twenty years does to Harbourfront."

"When did you learn so much about structural engineering?"

"Living on sand that continues to settle scares me. I want something solid under my feet," Holly said.

Virtue sighed.

"Are you helping with the flyer campaign this morning?"

"Yes," said Virtue.

"I told Gwen I was sick. I am about to betray everything she stands for. What if I get caught?"

A CROWD HAD GATHERED in the gym of the West Neighbourhood House, formerly known as St. Christopher House, but any reference to anything Christian was decidedly out of vogue in this neighbourhood; even the Portuguese teller at the bank, who always wore a gold cross with a fully crucified miniature muscular Jesus, tucked her crucifix inside her blouse now. Gwen stood near Nathaniel, the two of them facing a map of the neighbourhood taped to the wall. The room packed with business owners, the local Carmelite nuns, concerned moms — stroller bags on shoulders and babies, in various stages of sleep, wrinkled and saggy limbs clamped in carriers, dangling like elephant's trunks. A contingent of protesters from the Narcotics Anonymous group, who held their meetings in the neighbourhood, were holding hands, reciting the Serenity Prayer with messianic flyers of their own. A generalized sense of euphoria rippled through the room, the buzz of those about to embark on a meaningful mission. Nathaniel, handing out flyers and maps to clusters of his missionaries, waved when he saw Virtue.

In line to receive flyers Nathaniel asked, "Have you heard? City Council has approved the building permit."

"How can we fight this now?" said Virtue.

"We can try to influence prospective buyers," said Nathaniel.

"How?"

"I don't know, but I'm not going to give up." He looked around. "I've been at this every day this week. I need a break. Would you like to go to the Aquarium on Saturday?"

"Yes," said Virtue.

ON SATURDAY AFTERNOON, VIRTUE took the subway to Union Station. The pedestrian walkway with floor-to-ceiling glass faced Front Street; in this vast space, she felt like a tiny creature in a fishbowl herself, observed by those on the street. Could they see how nervous she was? Even though there had been a few pursuers: a beer supplier, the oyster shucker, and the bartender at the bluegrass bar. All of whom she'd turned down, pretending to be occupied with the demands of the restaurant, when, really, she was nervous, afraid of men like Holly's ex-husband, Gwen's lover, and the last man she dated, whom she, too, found sleeping with someone else.

But there was something special about Nathaniel. Something she felt she could trust, as if his zealousness was an extension of qualities that verged on the loyalty-above-all-else end of things in the continuum of human behaviour.

At the Aquarium, they stood in front of tanks filled with colourful tropical fish, mile-high sea kelp, and chunks of algae-covered rocks, Virtue felt Nathaniel watching her reflection in the glass and she smiled. In the jellyfish section, electric-blue lighting illuminating the sea nettle wall flooded their faces royal blue. The wall turned pink and the sea nettles, lit anew, darted in and out of the frame. They stood side by side, mesmerized by the aquatic life, passing through dark passages from one display to another. On the moving floor through the Dangerous Tunnel, they marvelled at the sharks. Three rows of teeth jutted out from blunt snouts. Lidless eyes peered at them and didn't and then did again. Prettier fish swam by: a variety of silver and yellow fish. A large sea turtle twirled on its back, wily fins flapping like a playful child. But Virtue couldn't take her eyes off the sharks.

In the kids' play area, Nathaniel poked his head up the glass viewing tube tucked inside the clown fish tank. A few dozen orange creatures glistened in clear water. Nathaniel posed as close as he could to the fish swimming through the water and Virtue took a picture.

The afternoon passed. It was close to three.

"Hungry?" Nathaniel asked.

Virtue nodded. They left the building and walked toward the lake.

There was a children's festival in full noisy progress at Harbourfront Centre, families crowding the sidewalks, children running up and down the wave deck, arms raised, screaming.

"So much has changed down here. There weren't half as many condos five years ago," said Nathaniel.

"It's baffling," said Virtue.

"Does Toronto even have enough people to fill these buildings?"

Over a late lunch, Nathaniel's cell buzzed. A text, from his manager, he said, and read it.

"Sorry, I've got to go. Another landlord on the strip won't renew a lease. Another business bites the dust."

Virtue watched him leave. She boarded the streetcar alone and went to her restaurant to help with dinner service.

LATER THAT WEEK, OVER lunch, Nathaniel pored over his cellphone messages.

"Excuse me for interrupting, but is your cause more important than time with me?" said Virtue.

"Our cause. It's just as important. But if my, our, businesses are going to thrive, we need to find a way to keep the leases on the buildings on the strip. Your building is now on the chopping block. The developers have made a bid on the property."

Where would she go?

She felt angry. The city and the developers were going to take her home and then her business. High-rise condo developments smack-dab in the middle of residential communities weren't the best example of city-planning.

Virtue overheard a conversation at the table beside them. The woman, asymmetrical haircut shifting over one eye as she spoke, whined about urban developments and the lack of significant heritage conservation. The man sneered at people who lived in condos. Virtue wanted to interrupt and ask them if they lived in a rental and if despite their politics they longed for smooth, clean ceilings like she did. Did they crave forced air heating? Were they content with lugging their clothes down six flights of unstable stairs to use washers that didn't work because of jammed coin dispensers — or, worse, robbed overnight, the dispenser ripped clean from the machine — or would they like a stacked washer and dryer inside their home? Nestled inside a closet? Tucked under the stairs?

But she calmed herself. Ate her salad and listened to Nathaniel muse about the possibility of her building being designated a heritage property until it was time to go home.

A FEW DAYS LATER, he showed up on her doorstep. He'd texted from downstairs and she descended the stairs to the front door to let him in. Walking up the crooked stairs, past walls crumbling from the weight of the building falling on itself, they stepped over debris of wall board, clumps of horse hair, Gyproc, and probably asbestos. The caretaker refused to sweep it in the dustbin and dispose of it properly. The expression on Nathaniel's face in the flickering light of exposed fluorescent bulbs fluctuated from polite disbelief and mild discomfort to outright disgust.

"It's repulsive," said Virtue.

Inside, an arrhythmic plunk, a hollow metronome, the sound of the leak dripping into the bucket. He walked into her bedroom and looked up.

"I've listed the property for evaluation. It may be designated as a historical building worth preserving."

"Would that stop the development?" Virtue said.

"A portion of it."

They'd intended to go out. Meet Holly for drinks. They spent the night in Virtue's apartment instead, the roof dripping over the edge of the bed. In the morning after he showered — Virtue apologized for the black mold on the bathroom caulking — he asked her point-blank.

"Move in with you?" she said.

"If you'd like," Nathaniel said cautiously.

"Let me think about it."

An hour after he left, Holly knocked on the wall. Virtue knocked back, twice.

"You stood me up," said Holly.

"What I got up to last night had nothing to do with standing," said Virtue.

"You didn't, did you?"

"Yes!"

"I met someone too."

Holly told her that some of the developers had met with Gwen to detail their marketing plans. Gwen didn't want to be the only woman in a group of men so she'd insisted her assistant join them. One of the heads of construction, Mike, showed up for drinks afterwards. They'd gone to Canoe. On the top of the TD Tower. Breathtaking views of the CN Tower and Lake Ontario. Virtue really should see it sometime.

"He asked to see me again," said Holly.

Virtue took the whistling tea kettle off the element and smiled.

"We stayed behind and talked until closing time. This is the first time since my divorce that I've felt anything for a man."

A week later, Nathaniel texted to say that he had tickets to see Elliot Brood and The Strumbellas. Two of her favourite bands.

The bar smelled like weed and yeast from the beer soaked into the cheap carpet. The dance floor was full of young men and women dressed in plaid, big eyeglasses, skinny jeans, and pointy shoes. Virtue had borrowed a Virginia Johnson dress from Holly. Two craft beers arrived. Nathaniel leaned in closer and Virtue turned towards him.

"I've put in an application for your building to be listed on the heritage register," he said.

Virtue said nothing. Her building was a dump. She frowned, then smiled. Was that the right response?

NATHANIEL CAME OVER AFTER Oyster Bar closed and stayed for the rest of the weekend, the pair of them nestled in bed, booking time off from work with nothing planned. The leak continued to drip through the plaster. It was cold with the boiler out. A storm started and the rain came. Out the sweaty window, they saw relentless sheets of water pounding the concrete in waves. They watched the news, shuddered at the thought of Lake Ontario rising, Toronto Island flooded and closed until July. At Woodbine Beach, the shoreline encroached on the boardwalk.

After Nathaniel left, Holly thumped on the wall.

"We've fallen for each other," said Holly.

"No!"

"He's the most incredible man I've ever known. There's a solidity about him that I hadn't expected to find."

IN THE MIDST OF the storm, extraordinary events happened. No one saw it coming. Blindsided the activists, the residents, the business owners, and the realtors. Especially the realtors.

"The developer walked?" asked Virtue.

"This happens when they can't buy up all the properties they want. Especially if one of them looks like it's going to be designated heritage," said Nathaniel.

THE NEXT EVENING AT the monthly Dundas West BIA meeting, Nathaniel took centre stage. He had new information. The developer was in financial trouble. One of the trades had put a lien on one of their other properties and when the developer paid the company it owed money to, there was none left and the bank froze their funding for this building. "There's a good chance the developer will abandon the project."

AFTER THE MEETING, A few of them, giddy with relief, got high in the laneway behind the bar that was popular with poets. In the midst of the haze, when the pot smokers got hungry, Virtue had a revelation about making kettle-cooked potato chips, in dozens of flavours, and serving them in barrels at an all-you-can-eat price at Oyster Bar. Now seemed like the best time, or would it seem insensitive to bring it up? Last Easter, her staff did not support the idea to have an All-You-Can-Eat Fish-and-Chips feast on Good Friday and call it "Sittin' Shiva for Jesus." They thought Portuguese families in the neighbourhood (or anyone else, really) wouldn't like that. She doubted current company would support her attempt to corral Suppies over to her Oyster Bar to get started. Suppies. She'd just dreamt it up. Stoned Urban Professionals.

VIRTUE OPENED A NEW text from Holly.

"How could she betray everyone like this?" she said, sitting at a table in The Communist's Daughter, Nathaniel across from her.

She read the text aloud to Nathaniel. *"Don't be mad at me. We halted the development. I've humiliated Gwen. If I'm going to be with a swindler better to be on the right side of the swindle. Love Holly xo"*

"You didn't have any idea she was leaving with him?"

Virtue hid behind the edge of her teacup. She was sure Holly hadn't intended to get so caught up in it all.

"If they get caught," said Nathaniel.

"The developer and Gwen must be going out of their minds," said Virtue.

"Would Gwen be vengeful?"

"I think so. She's worried about her reputation. Even offered to help me buy a house in the neighbourhood. She's eager to restore her reputation and distance herself from this project. She said she'll help me get a Family and Friends mortgage. Us."

"Us?"

"I've thought a lot about us moving in together," said Virtue. It was late afternoon and the light was perfect inside The Communist's Daughter; sliced by mid-rise buildings, the streetcar shelter, and five o'clock traffic; it fell over the tables. "And I want to. I think we should."

"I'm glad. You're going to need to move anyway. I got a letter this morning from the City. Your building was evaluated. They aren't designating it a heritage property. They're condemning it."

# *Adamantine*

WE BUY YOUR DIAMONDS flashed in neon across the shop window. Lindsay took the diamond ring out of her purse. It was a pear-shaped stone, framed by a cluster of black diamonds. She'd found it this morning in the soap dish. Her friend Stella had removed it to wash her hands, after making a mess of herself, spooning raspberries and cream over ladyfingers after the main course of last night's dinner party.

"Forgive me for what I'm about to do," Lindsay whispered. "I'll pay you back. As soon as this is over, I'll buy your ring back. It's a short-term loan, that's all. I'm not stealing this from you; it's just a temporary loan." She didn't expect anyone to understand. She knew what she looked like. A spoiled petulant upper-middle class woman, obsessed with having the best, willing to steal from a friend to get it. But she was trying to save her family. And save them she would.

THE DAY BEFORE THE dinner party she'd spent the day painting. Finding deep solace in the unfettered joys of her studio: the scent of acrylics mixed with the fresh peonies, pert in a blue glass vase on the windowsill, the vibrant blues on her palette and the pleasure in adding a perfect, terse brushstroke to a painting of a river washing over decaying automobile parts she'd been working on. Her husband Daniel had remodeled the space for her, not long after Oliver had been born, just after Daniel was offered tenure at the University of Windsor and she thought all of the initial problems in their marriage had gone away.

And when she'd had some time to herself, like she'd had yesterday before her friends had shown up for their monthly supper club party, she'd sneak away to indulge herself. A modest space — one small east-facing window, vaulted ceiling, old, splintered, paint-splattered hardwood floors — but she treasured it. The walls displayed some of her finest unsold pieces. The one with baby Oliver naked in the backyard — he'd snuck out while she was running a bath — serviceberries squashed between toes; a twelve-year-old Oliver on the honey-pink Dunalino pony, named Cinnamon, whom he rode at the Cider Mill Riding Camp in the summer. In a white cotton shirt, black riding helmet and brown jodhpurs, his legs clamped to the pony's flanks as it carried him over the fence effortlessly. And the portrait of Daniel, her favourite, one of the first she'd hung. He was eating an orange on the shores of Lake Erie — Port Dover it may have been, she couldn't remember now — to his left a tree-covered expanse of land that jutted out into the lake which may have led to Turkey Point. Muted tones throughout the painting, in his ginger hair, the fruit, and the setting sun in the distance. He'd looked his best in that portrait. She'd painted it the summer they fell in love.

SHE WASN'T SURE AT first if she could love him. She'd been dating a writer. A quiet, sensitive poet whose worldview seemed more aligned with hers than this man who thought only of economics. They were twenty-five, more than twenty years ago now, and he took her for dinner at one of those new Indian restaurants that had just opened in Windsor, after which they took a romantic walk on the boardwalk. The humidity was thick that summer and the wind from the Detroit River felt cool on their faces. She wanted nothing more than to jump in. She told him about a series of paintings she was working on that featured the river. He had a different perspective. For him its great glory relied on its business function — a highly-used shipping channel that kept businesses running smoothly for over a century, he'd said. He rattled off figures: the number of ships that pass through each year, the tonnage of cargo they carry, the amount of gas, and the cost that it took to fuel each ship.

"You're boring me," she'd said brazenly.

He stopped talking, blushed, and changed tack. He asked her about her master's degree program. She said she'd love to go for a swim and peeled the blouse free from the sweaty skin on her back.

"I know just the place," he'd said.

At his parents' house he stripped bare and dove in the pool. The cool water sprayed from his orange hair when he pushed it back from his forehead. His chest was covered with soft red hair. The ginger freckles on his nose glistened with water droplets. He swam underwater and splashed with his arms when he surfaced. He begged her to come in. She hesitated, unsure of what to do. Would she be looked at as coming on too strong? Desire rose in her, a balloon inflating, hopeful, buoyant and light, a surge of emotion she hadn't expected as she watched him. She felt safe. She wanted him to touch her. She slipped off her clothes and joined him in the deep end.

SHE HEARD HIM RUNNING the water in the kitchen. She put her brush down, irritated at the interruption — she'd just captured the movement of a wave perfectly — and wiped her hands. She placed her smock on a coat hanger screwed to the back of the door. The muscle in her leg crunched as she walked down the stairs. It had tightened as she sat painting; she ought to have remembered to stretch.

In the kitchen, Oliver stood with a glass of ice water in hand. "Sweet Jesus," he said as he lifted the lid from the crock pot.

"You don't have to eat the feet," Lindsay said.

"Aren't you going to clip the claws at least?" he said and made a sour face.

Lindsay reminded him of how much Stella, John's latest fiancé, loved Caribbean food, and she'd be dammed if she couldn't show Stella that she knew a thing or two about international cuisine. Chicken Foot Soup it was.

"Are you staying?" Lindsay asked.

"No. I just came by to see if Dad was here."

"He's not at work?"

Oliver said no. Said he'd left the Great Lakes Institute for Environmental Research and had headed over to the Odette School of Business, but he wasn't in a lecture or in his office. "He told me he'd put my next tuition installment in the bank today, but he hasn't."

Oliver needed the money for a work-study summer placement. The Institute was sending three of its top students to the Northwest Territories to study the recent discovery of microscopic diamonds at the Ekati mine. He'd told her that water droplets trapped inside the diamonds gave environmentalists a better idea of how seawater and carbon in rock formed them, ultimately giving them a stronger sense of how water and carbon cycled through the earth. He couldn't wait to go. All he needed to do was make sure his academic fees were paid and pay for his flight, rent, and food.

"I'll transfer the money today," Lindsay said.

After she made him a tuna sandwich and listened as he told her more about his summer placement, Lindsay went to the den and turned on the computer. She stared at the numbers for their joint account. Her mouth fell open. She scanned the page and saw the numbers against their line-of-credit and credit cards. He was at it again. After all they'd been through. After all the money he'd lost and the time she'd spent, tirelessly rebuilding their finances, working long hours taking on extra projects. He'd promised. He'd promised five years ago he'd never put her through all of that again. They'd almost lost the house. How could he do this to her? She must be somewhat to blame. She'd pressured him to put heated ceramic tiles in the kitchen, persuaded him to buy the Lexus last year, and asked him to consider buying a cottage on Lake Erie.

She opened a new window on the computer and called up her account, held at a separate bank. She ran her fingers down her face and rested her chin in her palms, her fingers wide over her cheeks. He'd found her card. The account was drained.

THEY WERE MARRIED ON a Saturday afternoon. Lindsay wore a cream-coloured slip dress and black boots. Daniel wore a white tuxedo and black sunglasses. John stood as their best man. He'd recently met the woman who was to become his first wife; she sat in a pew with their parents and a few family members and signed the marriage certificate, with John as a witness. The two couples went for wings and beer after the ceremony then crossed the border to see a Cranberries concert in Detroit. After the concert they raided the dessert bar at Casino Windsor. Daniel held a cupcake to her mouth and John took a picture. They gorged themselves on Nanaimo bars, bite-sized morsels of cherry cheesecake, and orange sherbet — Daniel's sleeves became damp and flecked with orange from leaning into the large white bucket to scoop the sherbet. They drank and played poker until six a.m., took the bus back to the rented house Daniel, Lindsay, and John shared close to the university and passed out on the living room floor.

HER MORNING SICKNESS WAS excruciating. The sour bile stung the back of her throat for hours. She hadn't told Daniel and she was almost three months along. He was preoccupied with doctoral projects and she'd just finished her portfolio for her master's degree. She'd written a final paper on the impact of industrialization on contemporary Canadian art. It focussed on Burtynsky's photographs and a few local artists dealing with, as she had, the environmental impact of manufacturing in the motor cities.

Lindsay rose from bent knees and flushed the toilet. She brushed her teeth, showered, and massaged her thickening belly with a soapy sponge. She dressed in a gauzy pink frock, tied her hair in a low bun and placed a wide-brimmed cream hat with pink cabbage roses on an angle over one brow. She'd found everything at the vintage shop. She wanted to look fancy. John had just graduated from veterinary school and had been hired at a local clinic. His ailing father had recently left him and his siblings his horse breeding business and they were going to the races to celebrate. Silly now, to think of what she'd worn, it was only the Windsor Raceway, not Ascot, but Lindsay wanted to make an event of it.

In the dining room, Daniel and John ordered wine. Lindsay picked at a few cubes of cheese. John joked that he'd rather have beer; the wine, cheese, and the dining room were all a bit too posh for his taste. John's first wife silenced him, pressed her fingers against his lips, already drunk on the champagne she'd been drinking since breakfast, claiming she loved the pretense.

A vein in Daniel's eyelid throbbed. A few drinks hadn't calmed him. Up all night, writing papers; and, in the morning, he had driven across the border to the Ross School in Ann Arbor. He hadn't taken a break in months, wasn't looking after himself the way he should. When should she tell him? He'd have to know soon, but a small part of her wanted to wait until it was bigger, a noticeable mound, so he wouldn't try to talk her out of having it. She knew it wasn't the best time, they were still living in the rented student house, but he'd get full-time work soon, the university already had him in line for a position.

Daniel rose to place a bet on John's horse. He returned, holding his ticket up with pride. When the horses left the stalls, dirt flew from their hooves. Daniel and John watched, energized, pumping their fists, hooting and hollering, saliva spraying as they cheered. Lindsay had never seen Daniel so absorbed. When John's horse won, they huddled together and stomped in circles. They ran off to place all their winnings on another race.

Enough money to buy a crib, Lindsay thought. John's first wife, an equine trainer, stared out at the horses and said John had some of the finest-bred horses she'd ever seen. She then told her a story about birthing a young filly earlier in the year. It was the most complicated birth, she said, we lost her to perinatal asphyxia. She asked Lindsay if she wanted wine. Lindsay had paled, put up a hand to decline the offer. John's first wife looked quickly at her abdomen and winked.

"Does Daniel know?"

"I'll tell him tonight."

Back from the betting wicket, Daniel's brow unfurled. He was enjoying himself, blowing off stem. No harm in that, Lindsay thought, relieved to see his shoulders loose and his gait light. Emboldened by his win, he told her he'd treat her to something, perhaps a honeymoon? They hadn't been able to afford one when they married last summer.

We should go home, she'd said, there's something I have to tell you. Daniel put her in a cab and promised he'd be home after a few more drinks, but he hadn't come home that night.

Oliver padded around under her feet while she painted — or tried to. The scrunching sound of his diaper was oddly disruptive. One eye on him, the other on her easel. He was still learning to walk; he'd manage a few steps, then he'd fall. Lindsay tried to hide her irritation. She hadn't painted in weeks, too busy changing diapers, warming cereal, pureeing bananas, singing silly songs, reading books, collecting snot, monitoring rashes. Endless, all of it. She hadn't worked since he was born. Declined a job offer at the art gallery to say home and take care of him. She hoped that she would find a job at the gallery when he went to school, but she regretted not taking the job straight away. The extra income would help. Now that Daniel was, well, out most nights. He'd bought the house, built her the studio, kept her and Oliver fed and clothed, but they had little spending money. And he was so cheap. He'd spend thousands at the track but wouldn't let her buy anything other than the cheapest clothes and No-Name products.

They were celebrating Oliver's first birthday. Nothing fancy, just their parents and a few neighbourhood moms and babies.

The weather had started to warm up over the May long weekend, so they'd planned to use the barbecue. She'd bought hot dogs and burgers at the No Frills, made a few cold salads, a pitcher of iced tea, and a giant purple Barney the Dinosaur cake.

Would he come home for the party? He'd been at the track every night for the last few months, leaving her alone with a teething infant while he indulged his habit. The man wasn't a drunk. He wasn't into women or drugs; he needed the adrenalin, the euphoria. A junkie for the odds. Dixie, he'd said in his sleep, and Lindsay was disappointed it wasn't a woman's name. She could compete with hips and breasts, but these beasts — owned, trained, and jockeyed by a handful of men — were no competition. Their world excluded her and Oliver. Vying for his attention: home, wife, son, and betting. Betting won every time.

The next morning after the party — Oliver loved it, he ate so much cake he'd thrown up purple icing — she woke to find that Daniel had come and gone. He hadn't shown up for the party. She'd told their parents he'd had an emergency departmental meeting. No one bought it, pitying her with soft-eyed glances, whispering when they thought she was out of earshot, but she'd maintained her poise; cooing at the neighbours' children, lighting the birthday candle, lavishing attention on Oliver, singing the loudest, passing the cake. All the while, panic, which had long ago deflated the bubble of hope and love she'd floated on when they first married, clawed its way through her mind.

She stumbled over a toy in the kitchen and wanted to kick the cat. She was on the phone dialing Daniel's office when Oliver's cries, which had turned to shrieks, demanded her attention. She hung up. She'd speak with him later.

THE SUMMER BEFORE OLIVER started school, the first creditor called. She'd cried after he hung up, worried he'd make good on his threats. She'd have to find money to pay the bills. Yesterday she'd found loose change at the park, scrambled to pick it up before any of the children did. She'd never felt so humiliated. She'd run out of coupons for groceries. She'd have to ask her mother for another loan. But what could she say this time? What excuse could she give? Her mother had harangued her the last time she'd asked. Demanded to know what Daniel was up to.

Lindsay made all sorts of excuses, downsizing at the university, which netted her a short-term loan; online fraud, which resulted in half of what she'd asked her mother for; and wallet loss with subsequent credit card cancellation, which got her nothing. Daniel had his own rationale. After this race he'd stop, John needed the support, just until the contract disputes at the university were settled and the resultant stress was curbed. It's exam time honey; I've got anxious students plying me with questions and demands. I need some place to go.

How about home? She'd said, but he ignored the statement. She'd told herself she'd get through this. She had to. In eight weeks, Oliver would be in kindergarten. She'd already called the gallery. They were looking for additional staff in September.

"HE'S HAVING AN AFFAIR," John's first wife said. Lindsay was stunned. They'd arranged to meet for lunch in the café at the gallery. At noon, Lindsay told her assistant that she was taking a long lunch, meeting a potential donor. At the art gallery for five years now, promoted to head of the fundraising department quickly. No one knew she'd already been a fundraiser, keeping her household afloat, in the years before she began work at the gallery.

"He left Austria earlier than me, told me there was something wrong with one of his prize horses. I thought I'd surprise him with an early flight home," John's first wife said. "In bed with a long-legged horse groom, and he didn't even stop fucking her when I walked in." She was leaving, taking half. Lindsay exhaled. That would be quite an amount. John had his own practice now, not to mention how well his horses were doing. Exactly how much was their house in Riverside worth? Lindsay wondered when the right time to ask her for a loan might be. She'd have to ask soon. The creditors had stopped calling. Not a good sign. She was sure they would have to declare bankruptcy.

AN ASIDE, A FOOTNOTE to the big stories of the day — a disturbing fluctuation in the car manufacturing market, a surprising win for Baltimore against the Jays, a traffic accident on Riverside, a shooting in Detroit, a robbery in Windsor — but it was a story that remained with her for a long time after its telling. Tacked on the end of the newscast, a mere ten seconds of television, life stories, or special interest. Lindsay wasn't sure what this section of the broadcast was called — or even if it had a name. It was awfully inconspicuous if it did. This segment was about something called "Trash the Dress", a post-wedding ceremony ritual. A professional photographer was hired and the bride would seek out a rustic location, where she'd roll around in the sand, frolic in a creek, or truck through the rainforest, hauling her dress up over her knees to reveal black rubber boots, or beige Timberlands with yellow laces. It had become a nation-wide phenomenon.

The woman in the news had her photo shot in the Gananoque River. She'd most likely stood on the edge of the river, dipped the hem in, not noticing at first how quickly tulle absorbed water. Waded in to her knees, twirled as best she could, hoping the camera would capture the spray. The mud on the bottom proved unstable, incapable of holding her up. The water snaked its way through the dress, adding so much weight it rendered her immobile. The river had sucked her under.

Seeing this on the eve of her twentieth wedding anniversary, when her own foray into marriage felt nothing short of a riptide.

There. Now. All things packed. Her suitcase full. Her own wedding dress? Not included. She would be gone by the time he came home. She'd found an apartment on the other side of town. Oliver, settled in to his first year at university, living in a rented house with others his own age, didn't need her or a structured, reliable nest anymore. He could look after himself. She was free.

The bank was primed for foreclosure on the house. Daniel knew, but had taken little action. Let him be the one here when the roof fell and they pulled the rug out from under his feet, to mix the metaphors sufficient to express her feelings. Lindsay was done. She took one last look around the house, the only house in Walkerville that hadn't had renovations in the last two decades, where there were knobs missing from the kitchen cupboards, the hardwood floor was scuffed and scratched. A wonderful home reduced to a dump through prolonged deferred maintenance in favour of Daniel's addiction.

When she opened the door, Daniel was on the doorstep, eyes red-rimmed and puffy, remorseful yet defiant. "I've been to the bank. We're not going to lose the house," he said. He told her John had come with him. Lent him the money outright.

"And how do you plan on paying him back?"

"I don't have a plan."

She stared at him in silence. He lowered his head. If she

didn't leave now, she would not leave at all. Bristles on his chin, smoky grey threads among the orange and red, made him look soft and harmless and rugged all at once.

"I checked into rehab," he said and told her about the program at the hospital. A three-week residency, he said and asked her if the bag she'd packed was for him.

"It'll take more than three weeks to straighten you out. You're a lost cause."

He told her he knew what it involved. He'd spoken to a man at the racetrack who'd been handing out flyers. He wanted to stop. He wanted to get better. Would she give him another chance? Would she stay ansd wait for him while he tried to understand himself and what he'd been doing, and couldn't stop doing, what had brought them to this point? Would she please give him another chance?

Over his shoulder a serrated cloud, flat and flossy, drifted by, she couldn't see the position of the sun. She assumed it was just after four, or perhaps half-past. She could stay and make supper. Fill the house with the smell of onions and garlic, pull fresh basil leaves from her terracotta pot. She'd make spaghetti. He took a step inside and placed his hand over hers. He rubbed her arms. He was trembling. She could unpack her things. Daniel pulled her close and sobbed. She pulled away and walked into the kitchen, took out the cutting board, knives, onions and garlic, pulled a few leaves from the basil flourishing by the window. By the time she had the sauce simmering, he'd already unpacked her bag and filled it up with his things.

SHE'D BEEN SITTING SO long in front of the computer staring at the desecration, the carnage that was their finances that she'd forgotten about the chicken foot soup. She should have taken out the bay leaf an hour ago. Her dinner guests would arrive in forty minutes and she hadn't started the entrée. She wanted to cancel the dinner party, call the whole thing off, how could she sit and pretend she knew nothing when all she wanted to do was throttle Daniel? She'd have to proceed though, make a simple entrée, not the roti she'd planned. Perhaps just grill the meat and serve it over rice. She'd have to. She didn't want John to know. Humiliating enough watching him prosper despite every sleazy move he made.

She couldn't bear it if his fiancée, Stella, knew. The twenty-two-year-old, smug and merciless, would mock them behind their backs. As gorgeous as she was, Stella knew little about the world, expert only at maligning and criticizing others. The first time they met, at the inaugural dinner party at John's house — it was Stella's idea to start the monthly supper club — Lindsay had told her that she lived near Devonshire Manor. The old Martin family home, she'd said, hoping for a flicker of envy as Stella realized that Lindsay and Daniel lived near former Prime Minister Martin's family home. But no such flicker surfaced as Stella, concerned only with placing stickers on their faces in shots captured by her smart phone, had no idea the former prime minister grew up in Windsor.

If Stella blabbed about their private life, it would impact Oliver. So no, she'd carry on, again, pretend everything was fine. The doorbell rang. Lindsay rushed to open it. Stella, in a pink sundress, blond hair in a wispy bun, handed Lindsay a box of ladyfingers. John strode in, placed his shoes in the usual spot next to the plant stand near the window in the vestibule, went to the kitchen and opened the bottle of wine he'd brought and took out four wine glasses from the cupboard next to the fridge. A mouse bolted across the kitchen floor and scampered under the stove.

"I hate to kill the poor things," said Lindsay.

"I always get rid of varmin," said Stella.

*Vermin*, Lindsay corrected silently.

The front door opened. Daniel. He entered the kitchen. His golden-orange hair hung in greasy strands over his tense and wrinkled forehead, there was day-old stubble on his chin. Lindsay turned away; she couldn't look at him. Silently wished he'd change his clothes, the threads from his worn shirt cuff were tangled on his wristwatch. He had holes in his socks. How long had he not been making eye contact? How long had he not been saying much of anything when he came home from work? She'd like to be able to pinpoint the moment she stopped noticing, or caring. Was it then that he'd reverted back to his old habits? She'd been in her studio, most likely not paying attention.

When she'd shepherded them to the dining room table, she took the meat off the grill, brushed it with a mango-lime vinaigrette and threw it on top of basmati rice. There. Perfect. When she placed the bowls of chicken foot soup, claws facing up, skin tough and wrinkled, on the table, her guests' eyes widened.

"My housekeeper told me that traditional chicken foot soup doesn't have noodles in it," said Stella, whiny and discontent as she unravelled a noodle from her chicken foot.

John wound the noodles on his spoon and told them that that was how they'd found the painter Tom Thomson — whose work was now showing at the gallery, all thanks to Lindsay who'd found a corporate sponsor willing to pay for the exhibit — death by drowning in Canoe Lake, fishing line tied around his feet.

"That's how creditors settled things in those days," he said.

Daniel dropped his fork.

Did he just whimper?

"General Motors just announced that the transmission plant will close and move to St. Catharines later this summer," said John.

"How are your thoroughbreds? Will one of them win The Diamond Plate this summer?" Daniel asked.

"Tip-top shape, but as I was saying a lot of people will lose their jobs," John said.

Daniel hung his head and picked up his fork.

"This will have an impact on enrollment in your classes," John said.

Daniel remained silent. Lindsay, embarrassed by the way he'd interrupted John, tried to salvage the conversation. "How are things at the clinic?" she asked.

"I can't do anything for a ferret with cancer. I told the owner his animal will die, but he authorized a twenty-thousand-dollar retainer for a hopeless treatment anyway," John said.

"Fools and their money," said Lindsay.

"Trying to save that weasel will pay for this," Stella said and presented the ring.

"It's beautiful. Congratulations," said Lindsay.

Stella beamed and fluttered her finger amongst a spread hand.

Lindsay glanced at the untouched bowls of soup.

"Dessert?"

In the kitchen, spooning raspberries over ladyfingers, Stella excused herself to go to the washroom. When she resumed dessert preparations, Lindsay went in to run cool water over her face. Stella's smart phone on the hutch over the toilet buzzed. She picked it up, with the intention of bringing it to Stella, but changed her mind when she saw the message. She clicked on it and read an entire exchange.

He told her that he loved her. Couldn't wait to see her again. Thanked her for the money she'd sent. No worries, she wrote, John's got so much he'll never miss it. Lindsay continued to read the messages. She figured out that Stella was having an affair with a yoga teacher she'd met while on a retreat in the Bahamas. She'd gone in February, and had in fact come back tanned and glowing, but hostile and sexually cold. (Or so Lindsay figured, watching her move away from John's touch and attempts at kisses.) Stella and her lover were building a Healing Centre on Paradise Island.

What to make of this? Were all of John's marriages characterized by one form of subterfuge or another? He hadn't learned a thing after the demise of his third and fourth marriages. All women whom he'd cheated on or been cheated by. Lindsay didn't want to know about this latest affair. She didn't want to play the role of sympathetic listener, to either party, this time around. Maybe there'd be something in it for her. Perhaps she could find a way to turn her fortunes around. If she hinted that John had cut his third wife off for cheating and made it known that she knew, but promised that Stella's secret was safe with her. Christ, no, she couldn't do that. Despicable. Low. She placed the phone back on the hutch and went back to the kitchen. Stella was whipping the cream with a rusted wire whisk.

"I have an extra set of teal silicone beaters if you need new ones," Stella said and dipped her pinkie finger in to sample the cream. It dripped down her finger and settled on the diamond. She took the ring off to wash her hands. They carried dessert and coffee to the living room.

After they left, and four bottles of wine were emptied, Lindsay asked Daniel, straight out, no hedging, if he was placing bets at the race track again. He nodded yes and told her he owed people a lot of money.

"What kind of people?"

"The type to tie me up by my ankles."

She remembered what he'd said years ago about how much he loved horse racing, the thrill of victory, and the joy to be had in uncovering a significant nugget of information gleaned in the past performance lines of the Racing Form or the Standardbred program that resulted in a double-digit winner. She still had no idea what that meant. Or the seemingly present intrigue as no two gambling excursions were ever the same. And the unparalleled tales from the characters and personalities who also called racing establishments their homes-away-from-home. Those were his exact words, this tirade of exemplary English, because the man, not short on intelligence or wit, could rhapsodize like a poet on the topic. He elevated it to an art by referring to it as equine theatre.

Playing the ponies had brought their life to the brink of disaster once before, and now he'd started again. Binging again, seeking to soothe the various crises at work, hoping that he could gallop through the tensions in life with the aid of the high-octane chemicals his own body, in a state of euphoria, produced. Once again she was left with the lengthy emergence from the quake, paying the bills, making mortgage and car payments.

"They've threatened me. If I don't have the money by tomorrow —" Daniel said.

"What are we going to do?"

"I'll win it back. I'll go to the track tomorrow morning, before work, and I'll —"

"Are you out of your mind?" And in that moment, she knew with certainty that he was. No one could profess sanity while living like that, singularly focussed on the perceived payoff from a correct guess in a game of chance.

In the darkened living room, the smell of wine, musty, red stain still bold on their tongues, it came coldly to her. He was gravely ill. Potted plants, lush and sprawling, clustered around window frames, on the mantelpiece, end tables, and a bookcase were in need of water. If they dried out, withered and sank into a hapless state, it would be her fault. Daniel's face, pained and exhausted, looked pinched, yellow, and puffy. A dried apple, he reminded her of. The ones she carved as a kid for craft hour with her mother. They'd put swatches of cloth over a stick for a dress and a kerchief over the top of the head. Old hags they'd called them. Witches. Her first memory of making something out of very little. She'd have to conjure something up now. Make something of their lives out of the very little that remained.

STEAM FROM DANIEL'S SHOWER still on the bathroom mirror, he'd left for work only moments before. She walked downstairs, into the washroom next to the kitchen. There, beside the sink, was Stella's engagement ring in the soap dish.

Four untouched bowls of soup sat on the kitchen counter. Curds of grease hardened around the chicken feet. A set of curved claws poked out over each rim. Her cellphone rang. It was somewhere on the counter of dirty dishes. She knocked over a plate of wilted raspberries to answer it.

"Have you seen my diamond ring? We must have had too much to drink. Neither of us remembers if I came home with it. John will kill me, he paid twenty thousand dollars for it," said Stella.

Lindsay tightened her grip around the ring.

"Has your housekeeper arrived?"

"Yes," said Stella.

"Didn't she take a pair of your gold earrings last year?" said Lindsay.

"I can't just accuse her," said Stella.

"I'll look for it," said Lindsay.

She studied the orb of white light, heavy on her finger. It made her skin shimmer. Platinum clasps clung to the gem like fishhooks. Bait that had captured Stella successfully: a bit in the mouth of her greed. Diamond ring still on her finger, Lindsay backed the car out of the driveway.

She drove the car to the Windsor Raceway. Inside the smell of dirty feet, vinegary and moldy, dominated. Wafts of that smell that she could only describe as dried urine on polyester slacks. Putrid. Despite the overpowering smell, there weren't many people at the race track at this time of the morning. An older man in a porkpie hat leaning on a cane, a skinny black-eyed boy with greasy hair and red blotches on his cheeks. A feral looking woman who scratched her scalp every thirty seconds stood by herself in front of a large monitor a few feet away from a dreamy-eyed woman in a wide-brimmed hat, grimy cabbage roses flat and threadbare, a pop can in hand.

She almost missed Daniel, cowering in the corner, a shadow obscuring most of his face. She hurried to him and placed her hand on his shoulder. He didn't turn around, but commanded her to keep her eye on 'Adda Boy. She didn't bother to watch the horse he'd just bet on, she looked down at him and he told her the story through twitching eyelids of just exactly how much they'd lost.

"It's time to go to work," she said and coaxed him from his chair.

"I took the day off. I've got to stay here."

"You don't have any more sick or vacation days this year. You used them all up when you had that flu in January." He was taking unpaid days off.

"I'd better get to work. Daniel?" He'd walked away. Straight to the betting kiosk, where he placed another bet with a fistful of coins. Lost or gone. Mad? He didn't say goodbye when she left.

Outside, she sat on a bench. A man next to her asked if her horse had lost.

She looked at him and started to cry. Tears ran down her cheeks. He pulled a tissue out of his back pocket. The tissue she'd been dabbing on her eyes held in mid-air when she saw that he was missing one of his legs. Oh no, they'd gotten to him. The people who lend money and then take body parts when repayment isn't made, oh dear, oh no.

"Lost it in a car accident. I went on a gambling binge when I lost my job at Chrysler last summer," he said and shrugged cheerily.

Foolish. Of course it was a car accident. They don't really cut off your legs, or tie you up by your feet, do they? She ran the pad of her thumb across her runny nose and asked him why he was still coming to the racetrack.

"I like to watch the horses run, it reminds me of what it was like to have two good strong legs," he said and laughed. "No, truth is I'm here proselytizing, handing out flyers for a treatment centre. A few years ago, I couldn't stop. Betting was my life. Who you trying to drag home? Husband?"

Lindsay nodded.

"Leave him alone," he said, adjusting his Detroit Tigers hat, navy-blue seams from the gothic lettering limp and grimy. "You can't make him stop."

She sniffed and thanked him for the tissue. He held out a flyer and she slipped it into her purse. She got back in her car and drove. Parked near Ambassador Bridge and walked to the bottom of the hill toward Sculpture Park. Down on the boardwalk, amongst sculpture, she felt peace. The contained passions of the plastic arts were a reminder to retain composure, to keep things quiet, to sort things out silently. The great dramas contained in these sculptures always inspired her to carry on, to bear it all with grace.

She walked farther down the grassy hill toward the lake. At the bottom, there was a bronze sculpture of four horses' heads with no flanks, propped up on steel poles, encircled by a trim hedge, called *Racing Horses* by Derrick Stephan Hudson. The text on the placard read: *The angle of the horses' heads and the three-dimensional power of the sculpture reflect the movement and emotion of a horse race ... suspended in time, they appear to be racing forward with power and beauty.*

She placed two fingers on one snout and cried. Is that what he was after? Power and beauty? She didn't want to know what he was after. She didn't want to hear excuses. Reasons why wouldn't bring restoration to their finances, their home, or their marriage. He'd lose his legs if he continued. She pulled the ring out of her coat pocket.

The phone rang.

"I'll stop," Daniel said.

He'd become a shell of what he once was, a caricature of himself, a sculpture suspended in time with all appearances of moving forward. Her shame so great it was a wild river of its own. Lindsay squeezed the diamond.

"We could lose everything," Lindsay whispered.

"After the Diamond Plate this summer I'll —"

He was impenetrable, will as hard as a rock, unbreakable, adamantine. If he wouldn't budge, neither would she. She couldn't let him destroy everything they – she — built.

Lindsay turned off her phone; time to take care of everything again. She trudged back up the hill, turned her back on the soft patches of sunlight over the Detroit River, glinting like steel in the sun. Rays from the morning sun formed a lopsided halo as they bounced off Detroit's Renaissance Centre, an industrial Madonna, swathed in a navy-blue robe of windows and glass surrounded by a crown of sharp spears of light.

She shoved the ring under the silk scarf in her bag, slung her pashmina shawl over her shoulder, smoothed her greying bob, and put on her black sunglasses. She drove onto Riverside. Turned at Walker Road, crept along Ottawa Street, passed a vacant strip mall, windows sealed with slabs of wood, and stopped in front of *The Old and New Pawnshop*.

# The Pier

"HAVE YOU SEEN YOUR father lately?" My mother asked as she pulled a Bee Sting — *Bienenstich* — cake out of the oven. I resisted the urge to snap *why would I want to see him?* The man was an utter fool. He was always watching the flowers in public parks, the way bergamot-infused tea leaves floated in a glass teapot, the quality of textiles in period costumes at the theatre. Colourful things mesmerized him; daily life and its mundane responsibilities failed to hold his attention.

The spring he met Iris, and whereupon absolved himself of family responsibilities, I was twelve. Every other weekend we drove to London from our village, Port Stanley, to spend the afternoon at the Grand Theatre, followed by a late lunch. On that April afternoon, Dad was up before anyone else. He took a long time getting ready, tied his greying hair in a ponytail, trimmed his beard and polished his wire-rimmed round glasses. When Mom got up, she parted her thick brown hair in the middle, carefully combed it back, and knotted it in a bun. Raised a Mennonite, she maintained a sense of modesty in the way she dressed and wore yet another one of her beige tunics.

Dad whistled as he shepherded my cat, Persia, into the basement. My precious diminutive Persia, grey like an oyster shell, eyes as blue as the ink inside my ballpoint pen, knew we were leaving. She hissed. She hated the basement and the waiting for us by herself. She made the most horrible noises, mewing and pawing at the basement door.

The drive from our bungalow, on a private beach on the shore of Lake Erie, toward London, wasn't too long. I was absorbed in a novel called *What Milo Saw* about a boy with retinitis pigmentosa who was going blind. He saw the world through a pin hole, and yet, despite his failing eyesight, was the only one able to see the intentions of a woman who sought to harm a member of his family.

Dad turned the radio to CBC One and Mom, nervous in the car, hung on to her armrest. The city scared her. She complained that the skyline devoured the landscape. She was afraid that the city would swallow her whole.

Once in the city, we visited Victoria Park. Underneath a monochromatic sky with clouds that blanched the horizon, Dad, the landscape architect, pointed out the flowers in the park and told me their Latin names. Mom, content by herself, reclined on the grass, picked blades from her tunic, and watched us as we explored.

After *King Lear* at the Grand Theatre, we went to a café nearby. Dad ordered Earl Grey tea and shortbread cookies. On that particular weekend, when we met Iris, she was serving. Sexy in a white slip dress and chunky black heels with frizzy hair, golden and wild, piled on top of her head. I noticed a necklace with a moon charm dangling between her breasts, quite close to my father's face, as she bent to set the table.

"You've got paint on your hands," Dad said. His eyes twinkled above the edge of his wire-rimmed glasses.

"I've been up all night. And I wasn't having fun," she said and winked.

"What were you up to?" he asked.

"Working on my latest painting."

She said she was looking for a beautiful garden filled with lady's slipper. She loved that flower. She wanted to paint them and set up a camera and record the other flowers as they bloomed. He offered her the use of our backyard.

Soon, she was around so much it felt like she was part of the family. I couldn't call her Auntie Iris, like she'd asked me. I didn't have much to say to her. I was too busy, silently resenting my father. He only had eyes for her when she was in the room. Mom and I were invisible. He glared at Mom when she offered tea, accepted her cookies wordlessly, but sat with Iris and talked about art and culture. Iris was coy. She crossed and uncrossed her long legs; the silver sunflower charm above her ankle glimmered in the sunlight. She rested her chin on the backside of her hand and listened attentively, as my father, hands tumbling over themselves, spoke excitedly. His cheeks were as pink as the coral bells beside him.

"You've captured the peonies marvellously," he said as he watched her paint during her last visit to the garden. While he admired her painting, I followed Persia as she chased bees that were bumbling from one flower to the other. I pulled mint leaves from their terracotta pots and inhaled the scent on my fingertips. I shook the stems of bluebells and made a tinkling noise to amuse Persia. I was carrying her around a patch of leopard's bane when I saw Iris sit down in a wicker chair. She'd put down her paintbrush and was relaxing in the sun. My father walked up behind her and rubbed her shoulder, then put his hand on her neck, and bent down. She turned and met his lips. He eased his hand down her dress and cupped it over her breast.

I turned and ran toward the house. Mom was at the desk in the corner, doing the books for Dad's business, a slice of steaming apple strudel beside her. She looked at my flushed face. I told her what I'd just seen. I was devastated. Tears rolled down my cheeks. She pulled her glasses off and hung her head. She waved her stubby fingers at me from beneath the sleeve of her dress, and told me to go find Persia.

MOM SPUN THE BEE Sting cake around and inspected it from all angles, "It's perfect, isn't it?"

I nodded.

"He's going to marry her," Mom said.

"When?"

"Labour Day weekend."

I stepped over Persia, asleep on the floor, and walked out the kitchen door to the backyard. The garden was beautiful this spring, filled with spring adonis, anemone, and basket of gold. He'd created a paradise. It's no wonder Iris came buzzing around.

Mom stayed in the kitchen by herself the summer he left — over two years ago now — and found comfort in baking. She was preoccupied with perfecting platz and rose early to gather raspberries from the backyard. The smell of it woke me up the morning she'd found the note.

"He's not coming home," she said.

He had gone to London to live with her. He was converting a storefront to an art gallery for her. She was going to display her paintings, landscapes, mainly, of my father's garden-paradise.

A YEAR AFTER HE left, he took me to an art installation Iris had done on what remained of the Port Stanley pier. I couldn't remember a time when it was in use. Mom told me they'd closed it when I was three. No one was allowed on it. I saw very little beauty in a crumbling crust of rock that slithered into the harbour from the base of the grain elevator. It was an eyesore, bisecting the clear water, in all its dilapidated, lonely grandeur. She was part of an artists' committee determined to revitalize the pier and see it reopened for community use.

She'd soaked the pier with water from the lake and as the moisture evaporated, hand-drew chalk outlines between the edges of wet and dry. *To witness the imperceptible process of evaporation and memorialize water's fleeting presence on ground*, her artist's note read. I wanted to make sure my father saw just how fleeting her presence would be, because I knew she wouldn't stay with him for better or worse. And it was up to me to create for worse.

A FEW WEEKS BEFORE their wedding Iris asked me out for lunch. She wanted to celebrate the fact that I'd be going to high school in the fall. But I knew she would talk about herself the whole time. I knew she wanted me to be excited for her, but after almost two years of cohabitating their nuptials seemed silly. I dreaded the "girls' afternoon" she'd planned. We had pizza near her gallery. I barely listened, smiled and nodded, as she told me about her wedding plans. After lunch she took me back to her office at the back of the gallery to show me her wedding dress.

"Don't you love the colours?" Iris asked, holding the burgundy velvet ball gown in front of her chest; violet, blue, and green leaf appliqué wrapped around the bodice. I nodded. She placed the dress on a chair gently when her cell rang, a medley of tropical bird chirps. She turned the ringer off and offered me a mint.

"I'm assuming you're surprised we're getting married after all this time?"

"Surprised you're willing to support him."

I took a deep breath as I prepared to lie. I told myself I was being creative, talking their language.

"He's losing his vision. He'll have total vision loss within the year. It sounds rough, but there are many sighted guide training opportunities. You can learn to lead him. You'll have to change a few things around the house, install sensors in his teacup. It's nothing you can't manage."

"He's losing his vision?"

"Don't tell him I told you, he's probably waiting for the chance to tell you himself."

Her eyebrows shot up.

"He has a degenerative eye disease called retinitis pigmentosa."

Iris was horrified.

"He won't be able to work in his garden anymore. He'll never see any of your new paintings."

"Oh."

She sank into the leather chair, crushing her wedding dress.

ON THE LABOUR DAY weekend when my father was supposed to marry Iris, the pier in Port Stanley re-opened. I walked from our house, through Dad's lovely garden, down to the beach and into the water. I was alone, except for a boat anchored twenty feet from shore. I was floating on my back when I felt a slight flutter, a tickle, where my neck met the water. I rolled and saw the brilliant orange and black velvet on the wings of a monarch butterfly. Its wings were spread out on the surface of the lake. Its black antennae were twitching. Treading water, I picked it up with one hand and let the water slip through my fingers, then I gently threw it up into the air. It fell. I picked it up once again and shook the water from its wings. When I threw it up this time it flew back to shore. Perhaps it was too weary to migrate across Lake Erie to Mexico, too frightened at the prospect of such a long haul. If it stayed in Port Stanley it would die. I pictured it, bitten by the first frost, antennae crisp, glazed by ice, wings stiff and candied, clinging to late-season coneflowers, and I felt a sorrow I couldn't quite understand.

My father emerged from the garden, goat's beard brushing at his ankles, dragging an Adirondack chair from the fire pit down to the lake. Where else would he go to find consolation? He'd been coming back once a week since he left. Mom couldn't deny him access to the garden. He'd created and nurtured the garden himself so he knew what every flower needed. It saved her time and money, she'd said. I'm not sure if it hurt her to see him so often, or if she looked forward to it. Did she feel as comforted by his presence as he felt being in the garden? She seemed happier since the wedding had been cancelled. Did she expect him to return, to reconcile?

I swam toward the shore, then stood in the shallows, and emerged from the lake. I walked up to him and sat on the beach beside the Adirondack chair. We were silent.

I took his hand and linked my fingers with his.

Mom sang out from the back porch, "Tea's ready."

Dad followed me up to the house.

"I was an utter fool to give this up," he said. "I've been contracted to landscape the new park that's opening up by the pier when they tear down the grain elevator. I can stay at the Kettle Creek Inn, but do you think Mom would let me stay?"

He walked up the stairs, smiling and full of hope.

She stood in the doorway, smoothing the creases in her pink linen tunic.

"Hello," he said.

I held my breath.

She closed the door in his face.

I couldn't sleep that night. I got up to make tea. The kettle, whistling while I sat nearby, immobilized, lost in thought, woke Mom up.

"What are you doing up so late?" My mom asked.

"Thinking about what I've done."

"What did you do?"

I lifted my head up and told her. Her eyes widened.

"Wherever did you hear about retinitis pigmentosa?"

I told her that I must have read about it somewhere.

"Wow," Mom said and tried not to laugh.

I was miserable. I wish I'd had the foresight to understand that Iris would break my father's heart. That his heartbreak wouldn't repair my mother's. It wouldn't repair mine. I shouldn't have interfered. I suppose I wanted him back, even more than I imagined my mother did. She'd loved him once, I thought, left the Mennonite faith for him. He'd lived in London when they'd met and had driven to Aylmer to buy soil, rich with horse manure, from the Mennonite farmers. She told me he'd tasted a butter tart she'd baked to sell at the Farmers' Market and his eyes had lit up. He'd flirted with her outrageously. "He saw sparks," she'd said. "I saw the possibility of an electric stand mixer."

She'd told me that the Mennonite families she'd grown up with eschewed the use of electricity, and that all she'd longed for was an oven that didn't use logs, spit sparks, or make the house smell like smoke.

When my father left, she wore her prayer cap again, and dropped the hemlines of her skirts by a few inches. On her own, she'd bloomed, reminded me somewhat of a plump rose with her light petal pink shawl over a pink tunic and skirt with voluminous slashes that served as pockets. She didn't, and wouldn't, go so far as to cut the electricity. Cut off from her baking, she would be lonely.

"When you see him again you can —" Mom said and stopped mid-sentence. She got up and brought my teacup to the sink.

I didn't know if I wanted to see him. I didn't think I could look him in the eye after what I'd done.

# What Follows the Falls

I WATCH THE MIST from my kitchen window. Coils hang above the gorge, white as a mountain peak, opalescent, dense. Deceptive, it won't save you if you fall. It can't carry your burdens. But I stare at it now, in the hopes of finding concealment in the vapour. I want it to swallow the truth. Hide what I've seen.

I suppose I don't need what she took. I want it. But I don't need it. She doesn't need it either, but she definitely wanted it. So she helped herself, crept into my daughter's room uninvited and rummaged through her closet. I don't need what she took, but it's a keepsake — mine to decide whether to part with or not.

I should have listened to my husband. He'd warned me when I met Amy eight months ago, said he didn't want her in our house. He must have seen something I didn't. Something furtive, sly in her thin lips and over-sized eyes, the way she ingratiated herself. Perhaps I'd been too harsh with her last night? I only raised my voice a little. I'm not sure what to do now. Should I, as my girls say, "ice" her? There are more things about her I'll miss than benefitting from her Target employee discount.

I finished washing last night's supper dishes, and set up my powder-blue Keurig. Dougal had already walked Duchess, our golden lab. The girls were at their Saturday morning ballet class. We'd finally get a moment alone. I'll tell him what happened.

I wiped the machine and discarded the pod. I was on the hunt for this coffee maker when I met her. Our love of coffee brought us together, and I wonder if when she said she'd do just about anything to get a coffee it wasn't a *proceed with caution* sign in and of itself.

I COULDN'T SEE THE red and white sign for housewares. I was lost in linens, fingering the hand towels, evaluating their thread count when Amy bumped into me with her cart.

"Sorry," I said.

Amy stared at the children's clothes draped over the crook of my elbow.

"Watch that Starbucks don't stain your clothes," she said.

"It's empty, but thanks. My girls will kill me if I stain their new shirts."

She bristled then sighed, asked if she could help with anything. I told her I was looking for a Keurig coffee maker. She left her cart, full of towels to be re-shelved, and took me to housewares.

"I like this blue one," I said.

She told me she had the same one. We bantered a bit, teasing one another about caffeine addiction, discovered we both liked our coffee the same way — milk with two sugars — and we'd both watched *Big Little Lies* on HBO religiously over the winter. And, despite her lack of exposure to the term, we considered ourselves irreligious. Give me your purchases, she'd said. And when I'd said, "Excuse me?" She'd surprised me by offering use of her staff discount. She could ring them through, no problem.

She said it was time for her break and would I like to join her for a coffee at the Starbucks? When Dougal and the girls found us, we were deep in conversation about affordable healthcare.

"The next time you cross the border, come and have lunch with me," said Amy.

Why not? I thought. It couldn't hurt. I'd enjoyed talking with her. It was so hard to find women to hang out with. My job as a copy editor kept me at home. I proofread city contracts from Dougal's office mainly — bylaws for daycare licensing, garbage collection, and zoning regulations. When the girls came home from school my evening consisted of driving them here and there, helping them with homework, and making their lunches for the next day. I had little time to socialize.

"Run don't walk," said Dougal in the car ride home.

Why does he always see the bad in everything?

"Something not right about her," he said.

"You're overreacting."

"She's a bit off. Her voice."

"Too loud for sure, but honey, we've got a lot in common."

So I went. Drove across the border from our house in Niagara Falls, Ontario to her tiny white house in Niagara Falls, New York — a run-down, empty town whose better days had passed, with citizens who personified long-gone glory as they wandered through the city, empty-eyed, weary, and determined.

It was a Monday afternoon. I took the day off and she did too. She was waiting for me at her front window when I pulled up. Once inside she gave me a tour: modest kitchen, cozy backyard, powder room with black and white tiles, airy living room. Her bedroom upstairs smelled like coconut. A plug-in tropical air freshener, she said, to hide the smell of her husband's cigarettes.

She opened a closed door at the end of the hallway to reveal a child's nursery. A gorgeous little room, filled with all the cute things Target sold. A white crib and change table, a bureau with a small library of classic children's picture books. The walls were painted peach.

"I didn't know you were expecting," I said.

"More like hoping," she said.

She told me she'd been trying to get pregnant for over six years. She was sure it would happen soon. She put the nursery together a few years ago when she thought she was pregnant. She saw no reason to dismantle it.

"Every week I change the sheets," she said as I touched the comforter with baby animals cavorting on a grassy plain, "no sense letting it get dusty."

I was impressed by her resilience in the face of a continuous cycle of disappointment — every four weeks for six years, dealing with that feeling of failure — yet on the other hand I found the whole thing strange. She chatted away as if there was nothing at all hopeless about her situation, led me downstairs for lunch, listing off potential baby names; things she wanted to do for birthdays; how much she longed to make sweet potato purees. She was so full of optimism that despite how odd it seemed, I rallied to her cause.

"Of course it'll happen," I said.

"Do you think so? My husband —"

"What do men know?"

And we traded stories about signs of pregnancy, which multivitamin had the most folic acid. Foods to avoid.

"Coffee," she said.

"No!"

"Yes. No more than one cup a day for me."

I held up my mug and we toasted her first and final cup of the day.

A WEEK LATER I sent an email suggesting we drive down to Buffalo and spend our next day off at the Albright-Knox Museum.

"What are we seeing?" said Amy as she climbed into the passenger seat of my car.

"There's a lot to choose from," I said.

I wanted to see the Operation Sunshine Exhibit by Buffalo-based artist and professor, Joan Linder.

"I don't want to see anything that's just splashes of paint," said Amy.

Jackson Pollock it wouldn't be then.

"Or anything made with coat hangers or toilets."

In the gallery I directed her to the exhibit room. It was filled with hand-drawn replicas of documents related to toxic waste sites in Buffalo, Tonawanda, and Niagara Falls. A bright orange book cover with the title *Salt & Water, Power & People: A Short History of Hooker Electrochemical Company* on nine-and-a-half by twelve-and-a-half inch paper hung on the wall.

"My grandfather worked for Hooker," said Amy.

Hooker dumped twenty thousand tons of toxic waste in the Love Canal neighbourhood along the Niagara River. In the 1970s, families were forced out of their homes as illness after illness took root in the residents. We looked at a hand-drawn copy of a radiation study paper.

"This is so sad," said Amy.

"Let's go to the café, eh?"

In the bright café, Amy told me she wanted to go to the Lily Dale Assembly in Western New York. A place where mediums channelled the dead, chakras could be cleansed, and, if you were lucky, you could hear one of the founders of contemporary Wicca give a lecture.

"They'll give me crystals to place on my belly," said Amy.

Did she really believe something external influenced something so, well, internal?

"And a package of cleansing teas to drink before bed."

Cleansing teas?

"I hope this will help me get pregnant." She wanted it so badly. I knew what it was like to want something and not get it. It's not as if I hadn't had doors close in my face while trying to conceive. I'd had two miscarriages before I had my first baby. I had faith in her. She'd managed to cut down on the coffee. I knew she could do this.

"Will you come with me to Lily Dale?"

"I'M GOING TO ASK my dead husband where he left the keys to the liquor cabinet," said the old woman and laughed, smearing mauve lipstick on her grey overbite. I nudged Amy, asleep, head nestled on my chest. She sat up and wiped her mouth. The bus pulled up to the gates of the Lily Dale Assembly. A group of women at the back of the bus finally stopped singing about rainbows and fairies.

"I want coffee," said Amy.

"Don't," I said.

"They can work miracles here," said the old woman and reached across the aisle to pat Amy's hand, "they helped me quit smoking last summer."

"I'll need a miracle," said Amy. She stood up, a gargantuan katydid in second-skin jeans, spindly limbs knocking against the backs of seats as she waited in the aisle while the bus turned in the parking lot. The Saturday bus had picked us up at six a.m. down the street from Amy's. I already felt tired.

"I can't get pregnant. Been trying for six years," said Amy to the old woman. She wanted a healing. She hoped it would help conceive a baby. I'd wondered how something as nebulous as a "healing" would help.

"Best way to get over your problem is get under your husband," said the old woman. The bus came to a final stop outside arched gates proclaiming Lily Dale as the *World's Largest Center for the Religion of Spiritualism*. We walked inside, stumbled over potholes on unpaved roads in our thin sandals. American hazelnut and bitternut hickory trees abundant behind houses. Pastel-coloured bungalows with signs advertising mediums hung out front. On one, a welcome sign with stout sunken letters burned into the wood that said *Come sit on my porch*. It was quaint. Welcoming. I might enjoy being here for an afternoon.

The crowd — mostly women, all seniors, except for a young blind man and his sighted guide, a muscular blonde in a Melvins T-shirt who fussed over proper handling of the cane — walked in groups of two toward The Healing Temple, a white building with Greek Revival–style columns. A woman wearing a plastic, pink laurel wreath and a white linen dress descended upon us from behind a plump rosebush. "Welcome to Lily Dale," she said, inserting the sound of the letter *h* after the *w* in *welcome*.

Amy grabbed both her hands. "I'm Amy and this is my friend Candace."

"I'm Athena, one of the spiritual leaders. I'll bring you to your session shortly."

She gave us each a strip of cloth and told us to place it on the tree with the other purple, blue, and raspberry-coloured bows.

"I hope this works," Amy said and tied her ribbon to the tree.

"I'm not going inside," I said and hid my bow in my purse. When she was inside, I spotted a sign for a coffee shop in the distance. I could go and have a drink while she was in the healing session. Amy would never know. I didn't get the chance because within minutes Amy came out of the temple, flushed and smiling.

"Let's get something to drink, eh?" I said.

We walked toward the café. Pink and spring-green cushions spilled out of wicker loungers crowded on the verandah. Wind chimes tinkled above. A handful of cats and a toddler roamed around the room. A barista held her arms open as if we were a crowd she wanted to embrace.

Amy ordered two lavender teas. I coughed when I took a sip.

"The healer told me to grab my fate with both hands," said Amy.

"You paid how much money to hear someone tell you that?"

"Don't mock. I'm going to see an astrologer now."

I accompanied her to the astrologer's bungalow. Her session would take an hour, so I set out for a walk. Paved residential streets in front of homes painted plum, red, and robin's-egg-blue. A personalized licence plate read *medium*. It was a community for the highly skilled; amateur mediums need not set up shop. The place gave off an air of authority. This wasn't just a circus sideshow. These were true believers.

I entered the Leolyn Woods. Purple pansies grew in patches around the pet cemetery. I was put off. I thought of the horror novel. Who wouldn't? I walked faster. Didn't dare look at the headstones. A blue jay fluttered amongst the blackberry thicket. My heart softened.

I walked by Inspiration Stump. A moss speckled stump encircled by a wrought-iron gate with bouquets of withered pink roses on the surface. Rows of pews faced the altar of the stump; they began to fill up with people, women mostly, who came for what they called the "One o'clock Stump." A reverend stood beside the stump and prayed. I slowly backed away as he thanked God for the continuity of the stump. I assumed he gave praise for the life cycle of the tree, analogous to our own cycles of birth, death, and the supposed afterlife. Notions of the afterlife were central to their doctrine. And what went on there? Did pets make audible noises? What about annoying mosquitos?

I checked my watch. Another thirty minutes until Amy was finished. I wandered a bit more, dying for a coffee, until I found the Fairy Trail. A white, undecorated trellis marked the entranceway. A handwritten note stuck to a tree read *glitter is litter please don't put it on the trail*. Did people scatter glitter here? In the hopes of what exactly — illuminating the spirits on the trail? Farther along, as the result of some ritual whose meaning escaped me, were fairy houses made of plastic, seashells, pine needles, and twigs. Some fairy houses had tinsel streamers while others had paper. It was flashy and loud and overwhelming.

I stopped at a large recess in the ground. A note posted to a tree explained that this was a crater where the fairies had once landed. I stopped to rest. Despite my lack of comprehension, I relaxed. Sunbeams like vines fell from the tree tops.

My girls would love it here. I thought of a spring day, not unlike this, when they were toddlers and I'd taken them to the falls. The mist over the falls seemed like an entity unto itself. We sat on a grassy hill and they played with my hair. They loved to run their pudgy little hands, rubbery and soft like plasticine, through my hair and put it in piggy-tails, as they called it, or pony-buns. My eldest said my hair had a lot of laughter, rainbows, and fairies in it. I thought her innocent comments charming. I wondered, surrounded by a fairy world created by adults, reflecting their hopes and dreams, if there was an innocence that the women who came here still possessed?

Amy had a childlike ability to believe. Would it help her become a mother? I stood up, stretched, and made my way to the exit. I found Amy waiting outside.

"She pulled the Four of Cups and the Two of Swords," said Amy.

"What does that mean?"

"One of us in the relationship wants a baby, the other one doesn't."

My brow crinkled in disbelief.

"Better I don't have a child with a man who doesn't really want one."

"What are you going to do?"

"At forty I'm certainly not going to start looking for a new man."

I suggested we have lunch down by the beach. Small crests of water luminescent from the sun, like soft butter curling under the pull of a knife, veered toward the shore and frothed at the shoreline. We took off our shoes and rolled up our jeans. We stood side by side on a rock and Amy hung her head. She was quiet for a minute or two. I saw a dead fish, hook hanging out of its mouth, rolling on the shoreline. Its guts were loose. It had broken free from a fishing line.

Amy's lip quivered and she cried. I grabbed her hand and pulled her gently back to shore. We sat on the grass and I handed her a tissue. She tore into a turkey sandwich, mayonnaise gathering on her lips. Earlier that morning I'd made sandwiches for my husband, two for my daughters and two for us — all the people I felt a sense of responsibility toward, the people I instinctively mothered.

"I JUST DON'T WANT her here," said Dougal.

Dougal's emotional aloofness coupled with a flagrant sense of superiority — both traits honed from his days as the bullied nerd in a blue-collar family — kept most people away. All of his various facades, however, melted when he was with me. With me he was soft, tender, kind, loyal, and vulnerable, traits I forget about when he was in this mood. We'd met at the Brock University Library. He saw past my stringy hair and out-of-style glasses, or so he said later, and saw gentleness in my eyes. I was hiding in the library, as I did almost every day before a lecture, because I'd never quite hardened myself against the bullying I'd endured in a similar family and felt safest alone. I felt a connection with Dougal I'd never experienced. We married shortly after. Travelled to Cuba for our honeymoon. Sat on a tour bus and asked the guide questions about organic farming, the "special period" in Cuba's history, Castro's policies, and the fall of communist Russia, while the others on the bus only wanted to talk about the quickest way to get more rum. We were complete nerds. But with Amy I didn't feel that way. I felt like I had something she coveted and not the other way around. I could expose her to art and she was receptive. I could talk about being a mother and she didn't make me feel stodgy. It wasn't often I gravitated toward others, but with her I glided straight into her open offer of friendship.

"I'm going to invite them," I said.

And I did. They showed up on a Friday evening after work.

Dougal agreed, not without protest, to attend my dinner party.

"Dang good coleslaw," said Amy's husband, Mike.

Dougal looked at me with wide eyes. Duchess sauntered in, thick tail buoyant, and begged for a scrap. Dougal took her gently by the collar and led her to the doghouse.

"I hate dogs," Mike said when Dougal returned.

Dougal stiffened.

"We get all kinds of strays begging outside Target," said Mike.

"Call animal services. They'll take them in," said Dougal.

"I says to my staff, 'I'm the manager here and we gotta do something about the strays coming to the dumpsters behind the store,' and staff says they already called animal services, and I says, 'That's not enough. We gotta get tough on those bastards —'"

"The girls, Mike," said Amy, putting her hand on the collar of his plaid shirt. My daughters weren't paying attention. They had tablets on their laps. When dinner was over, they excused themselves and left the table with a plate of cookies.

"Those animals are vulnerable," said Dougal.

"I put baking powder on bread. When I was young, we fed seagulls baking powder on bread and watched them explode —"

"You did what?" growled Dougal.

"More water?" I asked, and jumped up to pour.

"And the dumb beasts didn't even smell it, ate it up lickety-split," said Mike.

Amy dropped her utensils and cleared her throat. Dougal put his hand over his mouth. Muzzled for now, I thought gratefully. What could anyone of us say? This was beyond anything I'd ever expected from him. I got up to remove the tray of chicken wings on the counter and placed it between Mike and Dougal. *Throw them a bone.*

Dougal snapped the cartilage off the end of a wing. Mike tore his in half and sucked meat off the bones.

"The next time they come to the dumpster, I'll —"

"What? Tell us what you'll do," barked Dougal.

Amy threw her napkin at Mike. I felt helpless in the face of this square off.

"Excuse us," I said. In the kitchen, scraping plates, Amy apologized and said she didn't know he did these things. I wondered, really, what she saw in him. Amy asked where the washroom was.

"Upstairs, end of the hall," I said and took the forks from her. I couldn't wait for the evening to end. I regretted inviting them. I peeped out from the kitchen. Dougal and Mike were in the living room. Mike had turned on the hockey game. Dougal sat on the edge of the sofa staring at Mike in bewilderment. Soon Mike would shout out for beer and chips and there'd be no getting rid of him. I loaded the dishwasher and heard the girls in the basement playing with Duchess, letting out a series of lazy barks that signified her contentment. I put the kettle on and set a tray with pickles, cheese, pretzels, and a party mix of chips.

Where was Amy? Gone for almost fifteen minutes. I ascended the carpeted stairs. The bathroom door was ajar and the light still on. I felt an awful feeling of disgust rise. Was she snooping in my bedroom? Was she looking at the things I kept on my nightstand? My journal? Our wedding photo? The dried rose petals I kept between the pages of my poetry book, the Pablo Neruda that Dougal gave me for Valentine's Day last year? Was she in the ensuite? Looking through our creams and ointments, our condoms and contraceptive foam? Would she be shocked to see that I did not welcome pregnancy? Actively tried to prevent it?

I burst into my room, expecting to see her bent over a drawer picking through my underthings, but the light was off and nothing was disturbed. I glanced toward the washroom. Again, no lights were on. And no sign of Amy.

I stood on top of the stair landing, convinced I'd simply missed her, that she might be out in the backyard, or had run out to her car, or joined the girls in the basement. Halfway down the stairs, I noticed that both the girls' bedroom lights were on. How many times had I told them to turn out the lights? I poked my head in one and turned off the light. I went to my youngest daughter's smaller bedroom and did the same. And there she was: curled up on my daughter's bed, a pink, flower-shaped pillow clutched in her arms. Her eyes were closed and she was stroking the pillow and smiling. She looked odd in the semi-darkness, bluish winter light long gone; navy blue sky casting a gloom over the room, made more eerie by her body, a stony grey figure lying in a rumpled heap.

"What are you doing in here?" I asked. A sharpness that I hadn't quite intended, but couldn't deny, pierced my tone.

"Nothing," said Amy and sat up and stretched, "only enjoying the —"

The what? Smell? Pink polka-dot bedspread? It was unacceptable that she was in here. I hadn't showed her any of these rooms yet. And when you enter someone else's house, surely the tour comes before the lay-down? Was it just me? Had she crossed the line? Now I was wondering if she might be just a little disturbed. This seemed beyond the parameters of rudeness.

"— quiet. I needed some alone time," said Amy.

I softened. That seemed plausible. After all we'd just endured dinner with her husband. I don't know how she did it every night.

"Why didn't you say so? I would have let you use my bed."

"This one was closest to the bathroom. I got a sudden pulsing headache in there. What kind of lighting you got in there anyway? So strong."

When she sat up, pink fabric poked out the front pocket of her hooded sweater. I saw the silver clasps and the gingham trim. It was my daughter's pink polka-dot onesie, the one she wore the day we adopted Duchess from the shelter. I kept those in a box in the closet. On the top shelf.

Disbelief contorted my brow.

Amy understood clearly the meaning of my look. "Relax. You don't need it, do you?" She stuffed the onsie deeper in her pocket.

She walked past me, strode down the stairs, head raised haughtily, looking back — and one look was enough — unapologetic with a small smile of triumph and entitlement. I remained in the kitchen for the rest of the night. Summoned to the living room only to refill the platter of food or dispense cold beer. Amy didn't look at me. Not once. She cracked nuts and jokes with my slightly drunk husband whose social remoteness softened while under the influence, when even the worst cretin in the room was invited into his sphere of comradery.

I coaxed the girls to bed. Put Duchess on her cushion in our room and crawled under the sheets myself. In the distance their voices folded in on one another. Bursts of laughter kept me awake just as I was on the cusp of sleep, until all was silent and I slept.

AFTER WIPING DOWN THE Keurig, I brought Dougal his coffee. I found him in the alcove on the computer searching for dog leashes. The phone rang. I saw that it was her. I ignored it.

"I feel for her," I said to Dougal who was distracted by a selection of retractable leashes.

"Why?"

"Because she's having so much trouble conceiving. I can't imagine life without our girls."

"Some people don't make good parents," Dougal said.

I was about to say, How would you know? You don't really know her. She might be excellent with children, but the girls had just come home. I could hear them arguing in the vestibule over the last coat hanger.

She sent me a text later that day and several more for weeks after that. I'd stopped answering her. Hadn't answered an email until she sent one, after many — too many? — that had implored me to contact her, filled with questions like *Where are you? Are you ok?* And the final one, *If you don't answer me I'll call the police* to which I responded with, *I'm fine. But I don't think we can be friends.*

And that was it. The last I heard from her.

A FEW WEEKS LATER, on a snowy Sunday morning in November, I bundled up and left, nowhere-bound, in need of solitude after a long night of battling a flu that had infiltrated the household. Clumps of snow driven by a sharp wind pummelled my face. There was a strange numbness in my gums. I must have walked for an hour, slush washing over my boots, dampening old salt stains in the shape of a wave, before I found myself circling back to town. I walked along the edge of the falls.

At the bottom of the Bridal Veil Falls, on the American side, frozen sections of ice lay around the chunky bedrock. Sheets of it inched down the side, frozen in cascading layers. In the distance teenagers climbed cliffs close to the pedestrian bridge.

Mist lolled over Horseshoe Falls — as thunderous as ever — and piped up the crest. I breathed in deeply, refreshed by its presence.

I trudged back up the hill, lonely without my family, a stiff cold settling in my bones. I'd have a coffee and then I'd head home. I walked along Clifton Hill, a crowded street with various ghoulish, adventure and gaming shops, and went in the Tim Hortons near the fudge shop. I drank my coffee and watched the Niagara SkyWheel — a modern attraction, larger than a Ferris wheel with enclosed gondolas, standing 175 feet high and the highest observational point in the area — out the window. Despite how many, if any, people were inside, it was always moving, oblivious to the presence of its occupants. It was cold, so of course no one was in line.

On impulse I swallowed the last of my coffee, went out the back door and bought myself a ticket for the ride. Inside the heated cabin, a muffled, high-pitched, instrumental version of the Beatles song "In My Life" played. I turned on my iPod to drown out the sound. A husky-voiced reporter on NPR announced an Amber Alert for Niagara Falls. It involved a Target clerk who'd taken another woman's baby. Witnesses say she offered to watch the baby while the mother tried on a dress. Identity of the suspect has not yet been confirmed.

Had she taken someone else's baby? If so, would the baby be in a car seat or in the trunk? A precious pearl hidden in layers of cloth, choking on exhaust fumes in the dark, alone, fretting for her mother's breast milk? Was Amy capable of going that far to get something she wanted?

I didn't know. I googled everything I could about the Amber Alert. I didn't find out anything new. There was a woman on the loose with a stolen baby. That was clear.

On the last go-round the wheel stopped to unload passengers. I was still high enough to see the entire expanse of the falls and the parks, the lights of Clifton Hill, and the brash casino towers. Rainbow-coloured lights over Horseshoe Falls blazing, flashy and loud, inadvertently cheapened the natural landscape; silence and drudgery and grey machinery on the American side. I watched the row of cars, exhaust and fumes shrouding the fleet of foot traffic along the Rainbow Bridge. Was Amy there in the scrum, her car one in a line of nondescript vehicles crossing the border on a drab and grey Sunday morning?

When the wheel brought me down, I walked home. Drained, empty of will and strength; frightened, too, about what she might have done to my girls if she'd had the chance. I'd find out soon enough if it was her. Part of me didn't want to know.

Walking along the edge of the Niagara River all the way to the hydroelectric plant and stopping near the mess of wires and cables and grey buildings brought back the afternoon we'd spent at Lily Dale. The bus had dropped us off and we walked the few blocks back to her house.

"What if he really doesn't want to have a child?"

"He says he does, doesn't he?"

"Yes, but what if he's just saying that to please me?"

"There are ways around a man's reluctance," I said slyly.

"Yes, but I don't know if I can be so deceitful."

She was an honest woman at heart. She couldn't even manipulate that slum-dog husband of hers into giving her what she wanted most. Apparently it wasn't a case of low sperm count on his part or an inhospitable womb on hers — or any other assorted afflictions or malfunctions; all was in order in that respect. Desperate times and all that, call for actions that seem like the best solution when you're fed up, pushed to the wall, and have exhausted all other, sane, peaceable options.

Suddenly she'd blurted out, "That woman's art, the water, its contamination, do you think it has affected generations of us women? Made it impossible to conceive?" I thought of the toxins, entities unto themselves, with purposes I couldn't fathom, surging through the water, falling over the falls, particles clotting in the mist above. I had no idea if they were related. There are things I'll never know.

I was amazed that she'd taken it to heart. I wasn't sure if what the artist had created for sociological posterity, turning scientific reports into art, was to blame but it fed Amy's conflict.

"Amy, you're overreacting," was all I'd said.

Her misty, tear-swollen eyes, not a drop escaping out of the bloated sac of her eyelid, looked forward as that American resolve, like an eel swimming, stirring itself in a current of static, ready to snipe at anyone who got in her way, made her bark out in a flush of anger, "Candace, don't tell me how I should feel. You don't know me at all."

# Acknowledgements

Deep gratitude to the Ontario Arts Council's recommender grants program for assistance during the writing of this book. Thank you to *The Saturday Evening Post*, *The Puritan Magazine*, *The Great Lakes Review*, *Crux* and *December Magazine* for publishing earlier versions of these stories. A nod to the Disquiet International Literary competition for an Award of Merit and partial scholarship to their writing retreat. Heartfelt appreciation for Michelle Richmond-Saravia, Jody Bellemare, Pamela Smith, Meghan Mooney, Amy Del Monte, Andrew Keenan, Mary Ashton-Toth, and Alex Hartnett. Your time and attention toward the book, endless encouragement and support were invaluable.

Thank you to my agent Cassandra Rodgers for joining me in this labour of love and to Marc Côté, for his wonderful editorial suggestions, and everyone at Cormorant Books for their efforts in getting this book published.

Thank you to Tony Dekker and The Great Lake Swimmers, for being the soundtrack that kept me sane while editing. The Drink, Swim, Fish initiative of the Lake Ontario Waterkeepers whose efforts keep our beautiful great lakes fresh, safe and accessible. Thank you to the Salonistas, who provided endless writing and publishing advice and support. Thank you to Joey, Karen,

Cynthia and the rest of my family for reading my stories and encouraging me. Thank you to Brendan and Bronwyn for putting up with living with the impromptu lectures on literature, creative impulses and moods of a writer — much love to you both.

We acknowledge the sacred land on which Cormorant Books operates. It has been a site of human activity for 15,000 years. This land is the territory of the Huron-Wendat and Petun First Nations, the Seneca, and most recently, the Mississaugas of the Credit River. The territory was the subject of the Dish With One Spoon Wampum Belt Covenant, an agreement between the Iroquois Confederacy and Confederacy of the Anishinaabe and allied nations to peaceably share and steward the resources around the Great Lakes. Today, the meeting place of Toronto is still home to many Indigenous people from across Turtle Island. We are grateful to have the opportunity to work in the community, on this territory.

We are also mindful of broken covenants and the need to strive to make right with all our relations.